Ordinary Girl

ALSO BY PAMELA GOSSIAUX

Ordinary Girl

pamela gossiaux

Tri-Cat Publishing

Visit the author's website at: PamelaGossiaux.com

First Printing, April 2019
Library of Congress Control Number: 2019903845

ISBN 978-0-9987669-7-3 (paperback)
ISBN 978-0-9987669-8-0 (ebook)

Cover Design: llewellen Designs
Editor: Roxanne M. Smith
Formatter: Dallas Hodge, Everything But the Book
Author Photo: Vera Davis Photography
Scene Break Graphic: Kjpargeter - Freepik.com

Published in the United States by Tri-Cat Publishing.

Tri-Cat Publishing

Dedication

To the survivors:
May God grant you peace on your healing journey.
And to those still lost in the world of human trafficking:
May you find your way safely home.

A note from the author:

Heather's story is fiction, but it is based on the true stories of girls and women who have been in the dark world of human trafficking. Because of that, if you have ever been a victim of sexual abuse, the subject matter and details might trigger some strong emotions. Please read with caution.

At the end of this book is a list of resources. If you're a victim of human trafficking or sexual abuse, or suspect someone else of being one, please reach out for help. Most of these help-lines are confidential.

Chapter 1

I sit on the edge of the motel bed and swallow the pill that will help me relax. My shaking hand sloshes the water in the glass.

I am scared all the time.

Fear is constantly clawing at my stomach. Sometimes it's quiet. Sometimes it shouts at me. The pills help quiet its voice.

There's a single knock on the door, and it opens. A man walks in and my stomach flip-flops. He is here early, and the pill hasn't had time to take effect yet. The last one wore off already.

I've never seen this man before. Sometimes I get repeats, but he's new. He's dressed in wrinkled khaki pants and a button down. He looks cleaner than most, but not by much. His dark eyes drink me in and he smiles.

"You're Heather?"

I don't answer him. Instead, I start to shiver. Even though it's warm in here, I'm freezing. The black slip I'm wearing isn't enough.

He hands me a crumpled up one-hundred-dollar bill. It's sweaty from his hands. I toss it on the night stand.

As he's unzipping his pants, I lay down. We don't talk. Most of them don't. Some of them try to. Some hit me a few times. (*Never* in the face. That will show.) Most just want to get on with it.

The motel room is dimly lit by a dirty lamp on the dresser. It doesn't matter. I don't look at him. I don't want to look at him.

He pulls my underwear off and presses himself down on top of me. The sheets smell of sweat and stale cologne and bodily fluids. He doesn't care. They never do. They only care about one thing.

I close my eyes and try to pretend I'm not me anymore. I try not to smell his stale breath on my face or feel what he is doing to me. It's over quickly, and this one doesn't want to stay. He stands, fixes his clothes and leaves. He is the last one of the day.

I lay on my back and stare at the ceiling above me. There's a tiny crack running across it. I wonder if it's from the weight of the people above us, pounding away on their own bed. I want to cry, but the pill I took is working now, so I don't need to.

— — —

Five minutes later Tommy walks into the room, opening the door so hard it bangs against the wall.

Relief washes over me. I'm glad it's him and not someone else.

My stomach does that twisty thing inside that it used to do when I saw Jake Willis in the hallway at my high school, only not the same thing. It feels a bit more like the other twisty thing my stomach did right before tests.

Tommy closes the door and stands there, staring at me, hands on hips.

He loves me he loves he loves me. The words pound with my heart.

Tommy is my pimp and he takes care of me. I hope he's not angry today.

He stalks over to the bed, and through the haze of drugs I'm starting to notice that he *is* angry at me. He *knows*. He knows I took the money.

"Slut!" he grabs my hair and yanks me into a sitting position. The sudden jerk hurts my neck. "Thief!" He slaps me sharply across the face and my eyes start to water. Part of my brain feels the pain. The other part of it is wandering around in the fog.

"I needed to buy condoms…" I begin, but he yanks on my hair.

"You only *need* what I give you, do you understand?" He sits down so he is right next to me. I feel his breath on my face. It stinks of garlic.

My eyes water more. That twisty feeling in my stomach is still there. I think I might throw up.

"Do you understand?" He shouts it into my face, his spittle wetting my cheek. I nod.

"Good." He lets go of my hair, and I fall limply back onto the bed. "You have to work it off." He gets up off the bed and finds my dress, crumpled on the floor. He throws it at me. "Get dressed. I'll drop you off."

I sit up and reach for the dress, but he sits back down on the bed. He raises his hand, and I flinch, but then he tenderly strokes my cheek. "I know what's best for you, right?" he says in a soft, overly sweet voice.

I nod because he does. Because he will beat me if I say he doesn't. The strap of my slip has fallen off of my shoulder. My right breast is exposed. Tommy puts his hand on the back of my neck and pulls me towards him, kissing me hard on the mouth. I taste blood from where he slapped me. Then he pushes me down and is on top of me. His weight is crushing me. I can feel his hands exploring, but I'm not really sure where. Part of me wants to fight through the drug's haze, to get up, to run. But the other side of my brain tells me to stay put. It's safer that way.

"You love, me, right?" he whispers into my ear. The stubble on his face is rough. His hand reaches down and unzips his jeans.

I can't speak to answer him. His weight is too much. But I know that he loves me. He is here, touching me. Proving it. He gives me things. Money. Food. And drugs to make it all better. He will keep me safe.

He'll hurt me He'll help me He'll hurt me

He pulls up my slip and I close my eyes, letting my mind take me somewhere else, giving into the pull of the drugs. They take me away, and I'm no longer aware of the man who is ripping out my soul.

— — —

When he is finished, we lay there in bed together, smoking. The joint he brought with him has something extra in it. I can feel it lifting me higher than usual. There's a slight tingling sensation in my head. I'm trying to explore this feeling when he rolls over and sits up, taking the joint with him. He extinguishes it on the wooden headboard behind us. I smell burning plastics, and now there's an ugly black spot in the fake wood.

Tommy grabs the crumpled one-hundred-dollar bill that is still laying on the dresser, knocking over the box of condoms in the process. Then he walks over to the chair and opens my purse, pulling out the money I made today. $1500. He stuffs it in his jacket pocket and zips it up.

"Get dressed and get in the car," he says. He leaves, shutting the door behind him. I find my underwear laying on the floor and put them on. Then I quickly pull on my dress. I'm a little wobbly from the drugs, and I almost fall over. But that's okay. They make it okay.

I leave and go down to the parking lot. It's dark outside. Tommy is quiet when I get in the car. He doesn't look at me and starts driving.

"I want to go home," I say, meaning the dirty house on Side Street that we live in. I don't want to beg. But I do. Because I know what's coming. "*Please*. I'll pay you back for the money I took. I'll find a way."

"You know the rules," he says.

He drives me to the corner of Burton and Straight. The shops are all boarded up. Across the street from us, a few people are leaning against the wall of what used to be a florist shop. They are smoking something. Tommy pulls up to the curb and stops the car. He looks at me. "Get to work."

I numbly open the car door and climb out. It's early spring, and the wind is cold and biting through my dress. The kitten heels I'm wearing don't give me much warmth, and I know that soon my feet will be freezing. As I shut the door, I look at Tommy one last time, hoping.

Please.

But he speeds away, leaving me standing alone on the corner, waiting for the next john to come along and buy me more time.

Chapter 2

ONE YEAR EARLIER

The day started out normal enough, with no hint that I would have a boyfriend by the end of it. Or at least a crush. *Me*. The girl who doesn't have time for boys or dating, because I'm trying to focus on academics. I want to get into Harvard Medical School and study neurology. With my already cram-packed schedule, who has time for dating? Plus, there's all the drama that comes with it.

So I steer clear of boys.

It's not that I don't have opportunity. Josh Meyer asked me to homecoming last fall. I agreed to go with him, but in a group, and I made it clear it was completely platonic. Brittney said I was crazy. Josh is cute, and a forward on the basketball team. But, whatever.

My morning classes are mostly APs, so I'm already loaded down with homework by the time I walk into the high school cafeteria and find a seat at our usual lunch spot. I reluctantly pull the bologna sandwich out of my lunch bag. It's all we had last night when I packed it.

Brittney walks over and plops down beside me, her lunch tray making a bang on the table.

Brit and I have known each other since preschool. We met on the first day, when I saw her walk in with ebony skin and her hair in beautiful braids all over her head. They were twined with purple ribbon, my favorite color. I had to have mine done that way too and begged my mom for weeks until she finally gave in. I came to preschool one day with mine done the same way, having no idea that white girls didn't usually wear their hair like that. We called ourselves princesses and have been best friends ever since.

I take a bite of soggy bologna sandwich.

"Did you hear Veronica was raped this weekend?" Brittney whispers into my ear.

"What? Where?" This takes me quite by surprise, mostly because I forgot and left my phone on DO NOT DISTURB all morning. I glance at it and there are about a hundred texts and Snaps. I'm such an idiot. But seriously, Veronica has been dating Kevin Smart for two years. They're exclusive. He'd protect her with his life. I think.

"At a party. The kids got drunk, and somebody drugged her drink. Next thing she knew she woke up in a back bedroom and her clothes were half off."

I immediately look around to see if I can see Veronica. Then I'm ashamed by my curiosity. Poor Veronica. I can't even imagine.

"She's not here," Brittney says, reading me. "Her parents are pressing charges. She may not be back."

This is sad news. It's our senior year and in just three short months we'll graduate. Veronica is a nice girl and gets okay grades. I'd hate to see her miss graduation.

"Who did it?" I ask, toying with the crust on my sandwich. My appetite is now gone.

"Some of Kevin's friends, apparently. They were all drunk."

I glance around once again. Kevin isn't here either. I'm trying to determine which of his friends is missing, when Brittney's boyfriend, Aaron, sits down next to us. Aaron is six-foot-two-inches tall (Brit measured him) and has light brown skin. He wears his hair really short and rolls his shirt sleeves up to show off his large arms. Brittney chose well.

"What's up?" he says, diving into his pizza, his appetite unaffected by recent events.

"Didn't you hear about Veronica?" I say.

"What? Yes. Terrible. But not Kevin's style. I'm guessing he wasn't around." He takes a huge bite and chews, his mouth now too full to speak. After a moment he says, "Pop quiz today in Mr. Montgomery's class, girls."

"For real?" Brittney says. "Are you kidding me?"

Aaron has Mr. Montgomery's class second hour, so at lunchtime he always tells us what to expect. I'm not worried, but Brit immediately pulls her calculus book out and flips to the latest chapter.

"You'll be fine," I say.

"Not sure about that," she says, reading over the textbook while she eats. I finish my bologna sandwich and pass on the blackening banana I brought with it.

The bell rings, and we pick up our books and leave the discussion behind. Just like the real world, our little microcosm has left the bad news of Veronica behind and moved onto the next new crisis: our pop quiz in Calculus.

I'm not too worried about it. I study hard because I want to leave this town behind and go to some upscale university. I'm really good at math and science, and my counselor says I should get some scholarships, based on my academic performance. I have one goal in life: to not end up like my mom.

Dennis joins us. He's the nerd of our group. He joined our table after Aaron stopped the football team from giving him a swirly in the guys' locker room during our sophomore year. Dennis apparently calculated a program to break the passwords of the football players' Gmail accounts. He cracked seventy percent of them. It might have been cooler if he hadn't used this info on a Power Point for his advanced technology class project.

"I predict Mr. Montgomery will put derivatives on today's quiz," Dennis says as we head to our lockers. I sigh. That's the one concept I'm struggling with.

"Did you hear about Veronica?" I ask, because he got to our table late. We've sort of adopted Dennis. He's a decent guy, but he doesn't really have anybody else. He can't keep his nose out of a book, and he's more interested in writing code than making friends.

"Yes," he says. Of course. Everybody has heard but me.

"People will blame *her*," Dennis says. "For drinking. For partying. They'll say 'if only', and the bastards who did the deed will be slapped on the wrist. Then they'll all turn eighteen and it'll be expunged from their records. She'll be forever changed, but someday one of them will run for office, and she can sink them on national television."

Dennis has a way of being precise. If not sympathetic. I close my locker and head to class, thinking about how Veronica's life is forever changed.

— — —

Turns out Dennis was right about derivatives being on the calculus quiz, but I think I did okay on it anyway. I have an appointment with my counselor now, so I head to her office.

"Heather!" she says brightly from behind her desk. Ms. Neilson's room is emblazoned in our purple and gold school colors, and she has inspirational signs all over the place.

I close the door and take a seat in the chair in front of her desk. *"All our dreams can come true…if we have the courage to pursue them."* is staring at me from a chunky block of wood sitting to my left.

"How can I help you today?" Ms. Neilson asks.

"Michigan deferred me." It's not a rejection, exactly. But it's not an acceptance either. It's a "let's wait and see if we get anybody better."

She shuffles some papers and opens my file.

"So U of C and Stanford have not accepted you. Michigan has deferred you. Still waiting on Harvard?"

I nod. My stomach flip-flops. "What if I don't get in?"

Ms. Neilson glances at my file again, as if she doesn't have it half-memorized because I've been in here so many times. After each rejection, I come to visit her.

She looks up at me, her eyes gone all tender. Like a sympathetic look will help me in any way.

"Realistically, I think you need to prepare for that," she says.

I wonder if she has even read the quote on her own plaque.

"But my grades—" I begin.

My grades suck. They suck and I know this.

"Realistically, A minuses and a B plus are just not enough for what you want to do," she says. I wish she'd stop using the word "realistically." The University of Michigan was "realistically" my last good chance. "Your ACT and SAT scores are remarkable, but not at the top."

Since when isn't a 1500 on the SAT good enough? Or an ACT of 31? How much more do I have to do? Stupid idiot schools.

She closes my file. "Heather, there are plenty of other good schools out there who would love to have you. And it's *undergrad!* You can work hard and reapply to these others later for medical school. It's not the end of the world."

But those "other schools" aren't options either, it seems. So far nobody has offered me a full ride. Small scholarships, yes, but not a full ride. We don't have the money.

"And community college is always a good start," she says. As if killing my dream isn't enough, now she has me living at home which I will NOT do and attending community college.

"I know you're disappointed."

"Disappointed?" I say. That's hardly the word. "But I still haven't heard back from Harvard."

"No. You haven't. And it's only March." She sits there, watching me. There's nothing else to say.

"Thanks," I mutter and gather my things. It's really not her fault. She's super nice and has been very supportive. It's me. I'm just too stupid to get in.

Chapter 3

I drive my 2010 Chevy Aveo out of the student parking lot. It's old, but it runs. Brit is riding with me. We stop and get a slushie on the way home. She likes to mix the flavors, but I always stick to Cherry Coke. It's my favorite. Why mess with a good thing?

"Do you work today?" she asks. Some of her slushie spills out on my upholstery as she tries to poke the straw in.

"I do," I say, reaching over to hand her a napkin from the backseat. My car isn't exactly pristine, but I try to keep him as clean as I can. "Don't stain Charger."

She wipes up the mess and tells me she is going home to do homework.

"Aaron is coming over later for dinner," she adds.

"With the whole family?" I ask. It's not like he hasn't met them. He and Brit have been dating since Brittney turned sixteen. Aaron is cool and really good to Brit. He's on the basketball team, the football team and is pretty handsome.

"Yes. It's Tim's birthday. Mom calls it a milestone."

"Oh yeah." I forgot. Her little brother turns thirteen today. A teenager.

I drop her off at her house, then head home. Before I get out of the car, I pull out my phone to read my emails. I do this about every fifteen minutes. *Please. Please. Please.* I pray as I open the app. An email pops up from Western Michigan University. I don't want to go to Western, but my counselor thought I should apply anyway. Just in case. I scroll through the rest of the new mail.

Then there it is. An email from Harvard. My heart starts to pound.

Harvard has been my dream since I was little. My great-grandma Heather went there back when they were first starting to admit women to their medical school. There's even a plaque with her name on it. I've seen it.

I breath deeply. Maybe, just maybe, it's an acceptance. My hands are shaking as I quickly scan it.

"We are sorry to inform you…"

"No. No. *No*," I murmur. Maybe incantations will make it go away. I squint at the type again. "…have to pass you up…."

I quit reading and close the mail app.

That was my last chance.

I sit there a moment, eyes closed, feeling the life drain out of me. It's almost like a death, this final rejection. The death of my dream. Of my life. Of all the work I've poured into high school and middle school and yes, even grade school.

It has all been for nothing. *Nothing!* Four years of studying my butt off. Passing up parties, not dating. Not even when I had that chance to dance with Jake Willis at last year's homecoming. Stupid, stupid, *stupid*, me.

Tears burn my eyes, and I open the car door. I will be strong. This will *not* crush me. I will *not* end up like my mother. I brush my tears away as I walk up our front porch steps. No time for self-pity. I can and *will* make it to medical school.

I unlock the front door.

I walk in cautiously. You never know what type of day Mom is having. Today must be a bad one. The curtains are still drawn in the living room, and her purse hangs on the hook by the door. She didn't make it to work.

This is *her* fault. If I had a functional mother, I could have studied harder.

I take a deep breath and exhale my anger. Then I walk down the hall and slowly open her bedroom door. "Mom?" It's dark inside her room, but I can see a figure under the covers, and the top of her blond head poking out. "Mom?"

She stirs. "Heather? What time is it?" She raises herself up on her elbow and looks at the clock.

"It's after school, Mom. Have you been here all day?"

It's clear she has. She's still wearing the same nightgown she put on last night. This is where I left her this morning,

11

sleeping. She doesn't go in to work until 11 a.m. so I don't usually see her before I leave for school.

She gives a little moan and lays back down. "I had a rough day, sweetheart. Tomorrow will be better."

Sure it will.

"I have to get ready for work," I say. I quietly close the door and lean back against it. I'm the daughter who doesn't exist on days like these. The daughter she can't care for. How I wish she'd ask if I got any emails from colleges.

My cat Gracie comes up and rubs against my legs. I bend down to pet her.

Mom is depressed. Clinical depression, they call it. It's not her fault, they say. But it *is*. It's her fault she isn't taking care of herself.

After Daddy died, Mom got really sad. That was normal. I was ten and didn't think much about it. She slept a lot and we had people bring over meals. Some days we would talk about Daddy and cry together. Some days she spent in bed, and I just watched a lot of TV and stuff. I eventually returned to school, and after about six weeks, Mom returned to her nursing job.

But she never really got better. The sadness crept back in to our lives. And now...

But I don't want to think about that. I have to get to work.

Pushing the Harvard email out of my mind, I change into some black pants and the signature "Cozy Coffee" t-shirt I'm supposed to wear at the coffee house. I grab myself a granola bar, pet the cat again, and head off.

My shift starts at 4 p.m. and I walk in the door five minutes early.

Mr. Sneeder sits at his usual spot at the counter. He's one of our regulars and comes in every Tuesday and Thursday evening to sip coffee and work on his laptop. He's middle-aged, graying around the temples, and wears a wedding ring. He's pleasant enough, and we always get into interesting conversations on a variety of subjects.

"Hi Heather," he nods, as I step behind the coffee bar and tie on my apron.

"Hi Mr. Sneeder," I say.

"How was school today?" He always asks. That's more than I can say for my mom.

"Surprise quiz in Calc," I say. He shakes his head sympathetically.

"Don't let the pressure squash you, Heather," he says. "Relax and —

"—have a cup of decaf," I say, finishing his sentence for him. We both laugh. He says this to me every time because I always come to work in a hurry, stressed from a busy day at school.

He's watching me over his glasses. "You okay?" he asks.

"Yes," I say cheerily. "I mean…I got the email from Harvard today."

He frowns. "Not what you hoped?"

"Nope." Tears threaten my composure.

He shakes his head. "They don't know who they're passing up."

I shrug it off because I will *not* be like my mom. Mr. Sneeder picks up his phone and starts typing in a text. I need to let him get back to work.

I walk over to talk to my boss, Jess, who is heading home for the evening. I'll work until 9 p.m. and then help Cherise, the shift manager, close up. Jess tells me the specials on today's menu and what I need to make fresh. We get a steady stream of people, and I'm busy for a while with the "after work" crowd. When it slows down, I mess around with the machines for a few minutes, then turn back to Mr. Sneeder. "You need a refill?"

He looks up from his laptop and nods. "Yes, please."

I turn to get the coffee pot for him. Despite his jokes about decaf, he drinks black regular coffee, straight up, for about two hours while he's here. As I refill his cup, I see three young men, about college-age, walk in the door. They take a seat over by the window.

Cherise is behind the counter with me, so I grab a message pad and head over to their table. They're trying to read the menu, which is written in chalk on the wall behind the counter. "May I help you?"

"How's the chicken salad sandwich?" says one of the guys. He turns his blue eyes on me when he speaks and holds my gaze, waiting for my answer. He's amazing to look at. He has blond, wavy hair that is parted just right and one side hangs slightly over his left eye. He's wearing a charcoal button-down, which he has open at the neck and rolled up at the sleeves.

He raises an eyebrow, and I realize I haven't answered his question.

"It's my favorite," I say, recovering. "It's made with red grapes that give it just the right amount of sweetness."

It's what we're told to say when customers ask. Jess has trained us all on the right descriptions of her entrees. But I blush when I say it.

A smile spreads across his face. "Sounds delicious," he says. "I'll have one. And can I have chips with that instead of the coleslaw?"

"Of course," I say, scribbling on my notepad so I don't have to look at him. Even though I could remember his order by heart.

The other two order Reubens and all three ask for iced teas. I retreat to hand in their orders, then I take their teas over to the table.

"Thanks," says the blond-haired demigod. He gives me a shy smile. My tummy does something funny, and I turn before he can see the smile that crosses my face.

I walk back behind the counter. Mr. Sneeder looks up from his computer.

"I think that young man over there is a bit smitten with you," he says quietly.

I can't help but glance over at the table. The cute guy is watching me, but as soon as he sees me, he drops his gaze, as if embarrassed.

"I think he's college-age," I say, because I can't think of anything else.

"Maybe. He's probably what, twenty? And you're seventeen?"

"Eighteen in a few months," I say.

"Two years difference. Not bad."

I'm pretty sure my mom, on one of her good days, would have a different opinion, but I don't say that out loud. Cherise puts their orders on my tray. I carry them over to the table. Suddenly I'm nervous.

"Thanks," blond-guy's friend says. "We're starving!" The friend grabs the ketchup bottle and squeezes some on his plate. "Want some, Cory?"

So blond-guy's name is Cory.

"Not on chicken salad." Cory brushes a lock of hair away from his eyes and meets mine again. "Can I have a refill on my tea?" he asks.

"Sure," I say. He has drained his glass already. I reach for it, but he's already handing it to me. Our fingers touch. His are warm.

I take the glass back over to the bar to refill it. I can't believe he's talking to me. And the way his eyes hold mine, like they want to know more. I bite my lip to stop myself from smiling like an idiot. My hands are sweating a little bit. When I return with the tea, his friend, the one with the ketchup bottle, says to me, "He wants to know your name, but he's too shy to ask."

I look at Cory. "I'm Heather." I once again try to stop the smile that is spreading across my face. But I fail. Then I feel my cheeks burning. What is wrong with me?

"I'm Cory," he says. He smiles at me. It makes his whole face radiant. "Would you, um, want to have a cup of coffee with me, or dessert, or something when your shift is over?"

I glance at the clock. That's an hour and a half from now. I remind myself about my self-imposed no dating rule. But what's the point of that now?

"Um. Sure!" I hear myself say anyway. "But, I don't get off until nine."

"I can wait," Cory says.

"Heather! Customers!" Cherise yells from behind the counter. I look over and there's a line.

"Gotta go!" I say and Cory nods. I hurry over to the cash register.

It's the longest hour and a half of my life. I'm so busy I don't have time to think, but I see Cory's friends leave after

15

they finish eating. Cory pulls out a laptop and starts typing. Probably doing homework. College homework. Every time I walk by his table to wait on a customer, he smiles at me.

There's a handsome college guy and he's flirting with me. OMG. Wait until I tell Brittney! But no, maybe he's not really that interested. Maybe I should wait and see. I mean, can he be? And I'm not dating because I have a no-dating rule. It's just one coffee. Just to be polite.

I'm driving myself crazy.

Finally, it's 9 p.m. Everyone is gone except for Cory. Even Mr. Sneeder left some time ago; I didn't notice when. Cherise locks the door.

"Go," she says. "I'll clean up. Romeo over there has been waiting a long time." She sets two decaf coffees down on the counter for me, and two pieces of our signature chocolate cake.

I glance over at him. His blond head is bowed as he's intently reading something on his computer. I guess I'm going to do this. I mean, what's the harm of a little visit, anyway? It's not like I'm asking him to prom or anything. I untie my apron and take it off. Then I go into the restroom. I finger-comb my thick brown hair and freshen up my lip gloss. Not bad. Not great, but not bad. I take a deep breath to quiet the butterflies in my stomach.

Will it bother him that I'm only in high school? What do college guys even talk about? What if I say something stupid?

I look in the mirror again and square my shoulders. It's just a conversation and coffee. That's it.

And then I go out, take the two cups of coffee and cake, and go sit next to Cory, while Cherise scrubs counters and pretends not to watch.

Chapter 4

Every year at the beginning of the school year, Brittney and I make a list of the top ten cutest guys at our school. Jake Willis, this cute brown-haired lacrosse player in our grade, has always been my number one pick. But I think Cory tops them all. And here I am, sitting across from him.

"This is really good," he says, taking a bite of the chocolate cake.

"It's Jess's own recipe. Our owner. She's makes the best food."

"I'd have to agree. The chicken salad sandwich was superior. How did you describe it? Just the right amount of sweetness?"

We both laugh. "That's what we're supposed to say. She makes us memorize the entire list of sandwiches, complete with all their descriptions, which she makes up herself. Of course."

"Of course." Cory smiles at me again. I notice he has a dimple on his left cheek. But only the left side. "I'm sorry," he says. "I feel like a dork. I can't stop smiling. You're just so pretty."

I blush and take another bite of my cake. I have no idea what to say. I could tell him how cute he is, but that seems stupid.

"Do you go to school around here?" I ask to break up the moment.

"Yes. I'm a sophomore at the University of Michigan."

Wow. He's obviously smarter than I am. He must have grades. And money.

"What's your major?" I ask.

"I want to be a doctor," he says. "I have my eyes on Harvard or Johns Hopkins for medical school. I know—I'm aiming awfully high! At least that's what my dad says."

"No! Not at all! I want to do that too! I want to be a doctor, and I was hoping to get into Harvard for undergrad."

But I didn't. I feel a momentary pang in my heart, but I push it down. I haven't gotten into Michigan either. I don't want him to know how stupid I am.

"Seriously?" he says, raising his eyebrows. "How cool is that? Well, if Harvard is your goal, I may have an "in" for you. My dad's best college roomie is a Harvard professor. Endocrinology. What do you want to study?"

"Neurology." *He may have an in for me?*

"Wow. The brain, huh? I want to be a vascular surgeon."

I can't believe we both want to be doctors! This guy is more than perfect. We launch into a nerdy discussion about science and all the classes that colleges require you to take in high school. He took like all of the AP science and math classes his high school offered, just like I'm doing. I don't ask about the Harvard connection. I don't want to appear too eager. Cherise comes over and takes our empty plates and glasses in the back to wash. I'm going to owe her big time.

"I can't believe your dad's friend is a medical professor at Harvard," I say casually to Cory after a while. "Wow. I mean, what are the odds? That's the top school on my list."

"Have you heard from them yet?"

I'm not sure how to answer that. I think of the email.

"That bad, huh?" he says.

I give a little laugh but feel my cheeks burning again. "Does it show? Yes. I just got my rejection today," I say, because why not? It's not like I can call them and beg them to change their mind.

"I'm sorry."

"There's still the University of Michigan," I say.

It's March. U of M has until April 30 to let me know. Ms. Neilson doesn't think I'll get in. I should probably read the email from Western. Most of my friends have their college plans figured out already

Cherise comes out of the kitchen. "Okay, fun's over," she says. "We have to lock up now."

I look at my watch. It's 9:45. Cherise took extra-long cleaning up so I could have time with Cory, and yet the time flew by.

I push out my chair and stand. Cory does the same.

"Let's go," Cherise says, her key in hand. She shuts off the lights and holds the door for us as we exit. She turns and locks the door behind her.

"Have a good night. Nice to meet you," she says to Cory and heads for her car.

We stand there, outside the door, in the cold darkness lit by the streetlights, and watch her pull away.

"So what now?" Cory asks. "Do you need a ride home?"

There are two cars left in front of the Cozy Café. Mine, and a red Corvette.

"Is that your car?"

Cory grins. "Yes. My dad gave it to me when I went to college."

"Your dad gave you...wow." *Yes*, I want a ride home! I want a ride home very badly. But I can't leave Charger here alone. How will I get to school in the morning? And I'm supposed to give Brit a ride to school. Practicality takes over. That's the problem with me. I pass up incredible situations, like this one chance to ride home with a cute guy in his hot car, because I am trying to be practical.

"I should take my own car," I say. Cory doesn't seem to mind.

"Okay," he says. "When do you work next?"

"Tomorrow night. Same time."

We are standing facing each other. For a moment neither of us does anything, and I think he might kiss me. I feel my breath quicken. His lips are so incredibly soft-looking. Is that the right word? Soft? I'll find out when/if he kisses me. Do I want him to?

But he only gives me that shy grin again.

"Well, good night, then," he says.

"Good night." I can't help but feel disappointed.

He waits until I get in my car before he gets in his. I start Charger up and pull out of the parking lot, wondering what will happen next. As I drive home, I replay every detail of tonight. It seems like it went really well, and he wants to see me again. At least I think that's what he meant when he asked when I work next. And he offered me a ride home. Was that him being chivalrous, or did he just want to spend more time with me? Is he into me? Do I want him to be?

And…my hands grip the steering wheel harder as this next thought crosses my mind… can he *really* help me get into Harvard?

Chapter 5

Whoever thought it was a good idea to have AP Chemistry first hour should be shot.

I sip my cup of coffee and try to comprehend the concept of chemical equilibrium, but the truth is, my mind keeps wandering back to Cory. I spent half of last night awake thinking about him and hearing Brit's voice inside my head saying "Girl, you *gotta* go out and have some fun."

But it's March and I only have THREE MORE MONTHS until I graduate. I can and will hang in there. No parties. No boys. Just study. I Googled "deferred" last night (since I wasn't sleeping anyway) to remind myself that the University of Michigan is still watching my grades. I still have a chance.

Don't blow it now, Heather.

Brittney's head is bobbing over her desk. Is she drifting off to sleep? The birthday party ran late last night because they all decided to go out to a movie afterwards. I was invited, but I was with Cory so ignored her text. I didn't tell her about Cory yet this morning. I'm keeping him to myself for now.

Actually, I'm going to forget about him completely. It was a fluke. No one like him could ever be interested in *me*. He's sexy, smart, and wow, what a car.

And he has a connection to Harvard. Not that it matters. That is TOTALLY not why I'm interested in him.

"Heather?"

I realize with a start that Mr. Mitchell called on me.

I scan the board quickly. He's in the middle of an equation. "Um...."

Brit suddenly comes to life and looks over at me. "Soda pop," she whispers.

"Soda pop," I say out loud even though I'm still not sure what the question is.

"Good example," Mr. Roberts says. "Thank you Brittney Roberts. Now can you explain why?"

Brit sits up taller in her chair. "Because the CO_2...is... gas..."

Brit is flailing. My brain is waking up. I raise my hand and speak before being called on.

"There is a constant movement of CO_2 from the liquid to the gas phase and from the gas phase into the liquid. But if you look at the liquid there doesn't appear to be any change. It's in equilibrium," I say.

Mr. Mitchell frowns. "Thank you Ms. Thomas. Maybe you and Ms. Roberts can win a team Nobel Prize someday." His voice is sarcastic, but I can tell he is pleased with my answer. Mr. Mitchell is a pretty cool teacher.

The bell rings and we head out into the hall. "Thanks," I say to Brit.

"Thanks to you too," she says, and we fist bump. "What were you dreaming about in there?"

I can't help blushing. I can't keep this from Brit. Not Brit. "I'll tell you at lunch."

Her eyes light up. "You got into Harvard!" she says.

My face must do something, because she apologizes. "I'm so sorry! Oh no. What happened?"

But the bell is about to ring. "Later," I say, and I hurry off to Spanish.

At lunch, Brit bangs her lunch tray down next to me and says, "It's a guy, isn't it?"

"What? How can you—"

"Because you never drift off in Chem class, and you're all dreamy-eyed. You didn't get into Harvard, and yet you're still that high on life—"

"It's a guy," I say and feel my cheeks heat up.

"What? Where? When? Girl, do tell!"

"Last night. He came into the coffee shop. It's probably nothing. It's just stupid." But I give her his full description of god-like looks and include the hot car. I don't mention his connection to Harvard.

"Do you think he'll be back?"

I shrug. "He did ask when I worked next. But I don't expect to really see him tonight."

Aaron and Dennis arrive. We talk about sports and classes and Veronica. She still isn't at school, and neither are Kevin or his friends.

"I heard the guys got suspended," Aaron says. "But it's not confirmed."

The day doesn't go fast enough. Brit has to work after school. She's a sale clerk at this high-end fashion store in town. Aaron offers to drive her, and so I head home alone. I want to shower and change before work.

Mom's car is still in the garage and the house is dark again. I hope we're not in for another spell. Mom has her "spells" and sleeps for days. Weeks sometimes. I picked up some groceries for us the other day so we're set for a long haul if needed. After the last time, the social worker told me I should call if this happens again. But I'm seventeen. It's not like I need a babysitter.

I enter the dark house, and Gracie greets me, purring. I pull back the curtains in the living room. "Mom?"

"In here."

The voice comes from the kitchen. She's out of bed today, but she's still in her bathrobe. She stretches her arm out for a hug, and I let her enfold me with it, but I don't hug back.

"How are you feeling?" I ask. Yesterday's dirty dishes are still in the sink. She's unshowered and her hair is a mess.

"I got an email from Harvard," she says.

Darn. I forgot we were sharing the account I originally set up so she could help me with applications and stuff.

"It's not a big deal," I say, shrugging. I open the fridge. "Have you eaten anything?" I'm starved. There are some eggs. Maybe I could scramble us up some for dinner.

"It *is* a big deal," Mom says. "Oh honey, I wish I could be of more help."

Yeah, me too. Maybe she should try taking her meds.

"I know how much this meant to you," her voice breaks. I glance at her and she's starting to cry.

Oh no.

23

I can't deal with this right now. I close the fridge. "I really have to get to work."

I flee to my bedroom and dig out my second Café shirt, the one that says "A yawn is a silent scream for coffee" and put it on. I brush my hair and freshen up my makeup. In less than five minutes I'm out the door.

"Heather?" she calls from the kitchen.

"Bye!" I yell to Mom, shutting the door behind me and swallowing the guilt. I should have made her dinner.

I keep my eye on the road and my mind on my job. I arrive a full hour early, but Jess is never one to turn away help. She gives me a bagel, and after I eat it she puts me to work.

Cherise asks a hundred questions about Cory, and I tell her what I know. Mr. Sneeder isn't here today. We're steadily busy, and I try not to keep glancing at the door for Cory.

"Are you expecting him?" Cherise asks.

"Who?" I say, playing dumb as I make a mocha latte. She rolls her eyes.

At 7 p.m. he walks in. His long, black wool coat is hanging open. Today he's wearing a dark blue button down with dark jeans and some Yeezys on his feet. Those must have set him back about $500. He jangles his keys in his left hand and looks in my direction. When our eyes meet, he smiles. I smile back.

"Prince Charming has arrived," Cherise says only loud enough for me to hear.

I can't believe he came! I hand the café latte to the customer and walk out from behind the counter to the table where Cory sits.

"Can I help you?" I say, giving him a little smile.

"Something caffeinated," he says. "I brought my laptop. I'm going to work while you work, and then maybe we can talk? Can I buy you dinner?"

We're open until 9 p.m. tonight. Dinner would be late. And I have homework.

"Sure," I hear myself saying. "I get off at nine."

We're really busy tonight, so I have to get back to work. Every now and then I glance at Cory. He's focused on his laptop, but a few times I catch him watching me.

Jess leaves at 8 p.m. and it's just me and Cherise closing up. I help her out and then finally, I'm free.

"All set?" Cory asks as I walk over to him.

"Yep."

"Where do you like to eat?" he asks. "I was thinking about this little sandwich place on campus called Juliette's. Have you been there?"

Brit and I love that place It's a great hangout to talk or do homework.

"Yes. Great food."

He pulls his keys out of his pocket. "I'll drive."

He opens the car door for me and I slide down into the cool leather seat. I run my hand across the dash. The Corvette is as amazing on the inside as it is on the outside.

It's cold and dark, but he puts the top down on the convertible and cranks up the heat and the tunes. It's only about a ten-minute drive through town, with the traffic, but it's awesome. People turn to stare at us and admire his car. Some smile and nod. Some give us looks like they think we're obnoxious, which I'm sure we are. I wonder if we are breaking a noise ordinance.

He finds a meter and parks at the curb, a block down from Juliette's. He puts the roof up on the car. "Stay there," he says, smiling over at me.

I stay in the car, wondering what he's up to. He jumps out and holds up a finger for me to wait while he puts money in the meter for parking. Then he comes around and opens my door.

"M'lady," he says, offering me a hand.

I laugh at this totally unexpected act of chivalry and take his hand. It's warm. He pulls me up and out of the car.

We hold hands as we walk towards the restaurant. His feels warm and strong. I remind myself that this is the first real date I've ever been on, but I'm pretty sure it's going to stand out as one of the best.

Chapter 6

We order burgers, fries and milkshakes. We make small talk. Cory is an only child from New York. All he says about his dad is that he sells real estate, but I expect it must be some big kind of real estate, like million-dollar houses or something. He's paying for college for Cory so his son doesn't have to work.

"I'm going home this weekend to see my dad," Cory says. "I'll ask him about his friend, the Harvard professor. Maybe he can help you."

"That would be awesome!" I say. I try not to appear too excited, but I fail at it.

"The Admissions Office is weird," Cory says. "Often it's not what you know but *who* you know. I'm shooting for Johns Hopkins myself, for medical school, but Harvard is second on my list, and I know for a fact that my dad can get me in."

"I'm saving Johns Hopkins for medical school too," I say. "That's why I want Harvard for undergrad." I take a sip of milkshake. "So what does your mom do?"

Cory dips a fry in his ketchup before he speaks. "She died when I was nine. Breast cancer. I really miss her."

Wow. I can't believe it. I so totally understand what he means. "My dad died when I was ten," I say. "Heart attack. He died instantly."

"It took my mom two years," Cory says. "She fought hard. She didn't want to leave us."

We're quiet for a moment. What else is there to say?

"Has your mom remarried?" he asks after a while.

"No."

"Neither has my dad."

The waitress comes and asks if we want dessert. We both say no. I'm so full I could pop.

Cory pays, and we put our coats on. "I'll drive you back to your car," he says. "I need to get back to study."

He drives slowly, leaving the top up. When we reach the Café parking lot, he pulls up next to my car. He leaves the car idling and looks over at me.

"Can I see you again?" he asks.

"Yes. I don't work tomorrow night."

"Perfect," he says.

He leans towards me and I close my eyes. This is it. This is the moment when he's going to kiss me. I wonder if I should lick my lips or not.

But then his lips touch mine and they are warm and soft, just like I imagined. He tastes slightly of the mint candy he had after dinner. A pleasant tingly feeling starts in my toes and travels all the way up, until it reaches my face. I wonder if he can feel the energy in our kiss.

It's a soft kiss, gentle, and then he pulls back a little. I open my eyes and his face is inches from mine. His blue eyes are staring into my green ones, and I can see how long and thick his lashes are. He's so beautiful.

His shy smile spreads across his face. "That was nice," he says.

I want more, but he sits back in his seat.

"I'd like to see you again," he says.

"Um, sure." It's all I can say. My head is still spinning from that kiss. I manage to give him the rest of my week's schedule, and we agree to meet up again tomorrow night.

Then he presses the button to unlock the car door.

"Good night," he says.

I say goodnight and float to my car, his kiss still lingering on my lips. He waits until I start my car before he backs out and drives away. I float on air the entire way home.

Chapter 7

In light of what happened to Veronica, The School Board thinks we should have an assembly to remind us about yes meaning yes. They situate it during second hour. It's a brilliant strategy, because the kids who got wind of it last night still have to show up to school on time or get marked absent for first hour. This way, attendance will be higher, and those of us who think assemblies are a waste of brain space don't skip it.

First, Principal Make-it-So gets up to talk. His last name is Makispow but since he reigns supreme at Galactic Central High, we call him Make-it-So after Star Trek's Captain Picard. It was Dennis' idea and it stuck.

Principal Make-it-So talks about sex and how we should not be having it unless both parties are in agreement. He gets into details about what yes actually means and what constitutes a no. He even puts up a Power Point with the definition of the words and how each separate stage of intimacy requires a specific yes. He's really gung-ho about this. I think he should print contracts up. We could carry them around with us, and both parties would have to sign before engaging in any mating ritual.

Then we see a short movie about "What is Affirmative Consent." After that, just to round it out, the DARE committee reminds us that alcohol and drug use is one way our "no" can be accidentally misunderstood for "yes."

We survive the fifty-three-minute ordeal and go to third hour.

At least I missed Spanish.

In third hour, our English teacher, Ms. Marple, decides we each need to write a short essay on respecting others. It's a broad topic. I can't help but think she was being forced to tie today's work in with the assembly. She gives us Chromebooks and we take off. Ready, set, go.

Lunch can't come soon enough.

"Well?" Brit says, now that we have a proper chance to talk.

"He kissed me," I whisper.

"Oh my gosh!" Brit shrieks. People look over at us.

"Shhh!" I say, busying myself by opening my brown bag. In a rare moment of parenting, Mom packed my lunch last night. I wonder what I got.

"How was it?"

"Nice."

"*Nice?*" Brit exclaims. "That's all you have to say?"

Bologna and cheese. At least there's cheese. "Yes."

Brit asks for details and I pretend to be nonchalant, but finally I can't hold it in any longer and I lean over to her and spill. I tell her about the dinner, the Yeezys and cruising through town with the top down on his convertible. Then I tell her about the kiss and his long eyelashes, and the fact that he wants to see me again.

"So cool!" she says.

"I know!"

But then she frowns. "So what happened to your 'no dating' rule? You didn't get into Harvard so now you're giving up?"

"No. I'm still waiting on Michigan. I just...Cory's different. School is important to him too. He's pre-med as well."

Then Brit suddenly changes the topic. "I have good news too!" She pulls out her phone and opens her mail app. She clicks on an email.

"Look! I got into Columbia University!" she says.

"I can't believe it!" I say, squinting at her phone. "I mean I *can*, because you're so awesome, but Brit, that's incredible!"

I'm really excited for her. That was her first choice. I'm also a little jealous. Even if they don't give her a full ride, her parents can afford to pay. They aren't rich, but they do what they can to support their kids. They planned for college while the kids were still little.

Not like my mom.

"Cory wants to take me out tonight," I say. "But Mom wants me to have dinner at home. I feel kind of bad if I don't show up because she's…" I don't want to say "she's finally out of bed," because then Brit will tell her mom, and there will be phone calls to check up on us. "She's expecting me. Can you cover for me? I'll tell her we have a really important project we have to do for class tomorrow. If she calls, you can tell her I'm there with you."

"I'm not gonna lie to your mother," Brit says firmly.

I sigh. "Well, then just don't answer your phone. I'll tell her we're shutting them off for an hour or two."

Brit frowns. I can tell she doesn't like this. She's pretty much a stick-to-the-rules kind of girl. But she doesn't argue with me either.

Then the bell rings, and I stuff the last bite of sandwich in my mouth. I spend the rest of the day trying to figure out what to wear tonight.

— — —

I decide on a soft purple sweater and skinny jeans. I have some brown suede boots that I got last Christmas, and I add those to the mix. My long brown hair is freshly washed and dried, and I leave it down. It's thick and one of my best assets. I'm happy with what I see in the mirror. Then I feed the cat and leave a note on the table for Mom. She is apparently at work today, so I leave before she gets home.

I meet Cory at the cafe parking lot and climb into his car. I decided I'm not ready for him to pick me up at home. Especially since I'm lying to my mom.

Tonight, he takes me to Carson's for a shrimp dinner. He pays again. The food is delicious and we stay for two hours, talking about school and our dreams. He really misses his mom.

This time he gives me a more lingering kiss in the car. I can feel it travel all the way down to my toes. I'm wondering what's next. Will his hands travel some place? Will the next kiss be more intense? But then he pulls back.

"Can I see you again?"

"Um…" I'm still reeling from that kiss. "Sure!" I say.

He leans towards me and we kiss some more.

"I'm going home this weekend," he says quietly in my ear. His hand is in my hair and I feel his warm fingers run through it. Then he pulls back a little. He's looking into my eyes. "I'm leaving Friday, but I want to see you again. Tomorrow night I have a study group at college, but how about when I get back?"

"I'd like that," I say. Then I open the door. "I had a great time tonight."

He smiles, his blue eyes twinkling in the light from the car dome.

"Me too," he says.

I take that as my cue to leave. I shut the car door and climb into my own. Once again, I swoon all the way home.

Chapter 8

I decide to tell Brittney about Harvard.

"Cory has a Harvard connection," I say at lunch. Mom has packed my lunch again. Today it's tuna fish and potato chips. She must have gone shopping last night. She was asleep by the time I got home.

"A Harvard connection?" Brit says, munching on a carrot stick.

"His dad's college roommate, and current best friend, teaches in the medical school. Cory thinks he can get me in."

Brit sits up straighter. "Oh. My. Gosh!"

"Yes."

"And you said…?"

I sigh. "I haven't said anything. I mean, that's the problem. I don't want him to think I'm interested in him just because of that."

Brittney laughs. "He looks like a Greek god and drives a Corvette and *that's* what you're worried he'll think you're after him for?"

I eat a potato chip. She has a point.

"So what do I say?"

"You ask him to get you in!" Brit says. "Duh!"

I think about it. I mean, why not? He's going home this weekend, so I should mention it. That way he can go straight home and ask his dad.

"Okay."

We see Kevin come in. He's not hanging around with his usual friends. I wonder who the suspects are. Rumors are it was Jake and Tyler, but they're both here today. Or is that how it works? The girl gets raped and has to stay home while the guilty parties get on with their lives?

Brittney sees me looking at them.

"People are saying Veronica was drunk," she whispered to me.

Aaron sits down next to Brit and kisses her. "Hey Babe."

"I see Kevin's back," she says.

Aaron looks over and nods, then eats half his hamburger in one bite. Luckily he bought two.

"I guess she was dressed sluttier than usual," he says around his food.

Brit frowns. "What do you mean?"

"Just what she was wearing," Aaron says around a mouthful of food. "The guys say she was asking for it."

"Whoa. Wait. Just. A. Minute." Brit says. She crosses her arms. That's a bad sign for Aaron. I almost feel sorry for him.

"What?" Aaron looks seriously confused.

"So you're saying that because of what Veronica *wore*, she deserved to get raped," Brit says. She has stopped eating and is staring at Aaron.

Dennis sits down with us. He heard the tail end of the conversation. He just shakes his head at Aaron.

Aaron still looks confused but has sense enough to know he's in trouble. He stops talking.

"Dude," Dennis says. "Think about what you said."

Aaron looks at Brit and then ducks his head. "What I *meant* to say, was..."

"Yes?" Brit is still giving him the evil eye. Aaron squirms. Even though I realize the seriousness of what he just mistakenly said, I can't hold back a smile. Brit has him wrapped around her little finger.

"I *meant* to say how beautiful you are today," Aaron says, and kisses her on the nose. "And that all women should be treated with respect. Even if they're naked. Especially if they're naked."

Brit elbows him in the ribs, and he coughs. But I laugh. Aaron is a teddy bear and he'd never, ever hurt anybody. Brit knows that, too, because she goes back to eating her lunch. Aaron just speaks before he thinks.

I think about what he said though. Every time a woman gets raped, it seems people want to blame *her*. It's either what she wore, that she was flirting too much, or that she was drunk; any reason they can think of. Like she deserved it. As if being too beautiful or failing to make wise decisions causes rape to happen. What *causes* it is are the men who do it.

"Aaron," Brit's voice brings me back to the discussion. "I'm making some posters for Student Council on 'Yes Means Yes'," she says to him. "You're going to help me hang them up around the school."

"Of course," he says. Because he'll be in trouble if he doesn't.

The rest of the day is uneventful. I keep checking my emails but so far nothing from Michigan. I guess in this case, no news can be good news.

Mom is home when I get there. She looks better than I've seen her in weeks. She's humming and mixing up a cake from a box.

"What's this for?" I say, sticking my finger in the batter and licking it.

"I thought we should celebrate," Mom says. "I'm feeling much better, and this will be the first dinner we've had together in over a week."

It's chocolate cake. I see a can of chocolate frosting next to it. Mom knows the way to my heart.

I head into the living room to catch up on homework while she cooks. She puts the cake in the oven and I hear her chopping vegetables for a stir-fry. Gracie tries to lay on my textbooks, which makes it difficult to work.

I'm behind on homework because of my dating. I remove the cat, open my calculus book and sigh. It's going to be a long night. I kind of want to tell Mom about Cory, but I know she'd freak if she finds out he's college age. Maybe I don't have to mention that. I can just tell her I met a guy.

I'm buried deep in equations when Mom calls me for dinner. It smells wonderful. We sit at our little table, across from each other, and dig in. It's chicken with a bottled sweet and sour sauce over it all, and it's awesome. Mom uses convenience foods, but she can make them tasty.

"So how is school going?" she asks.

"Fine."

"Any more news about colleges?"

"Nope."

I spear a piece of chicken and look closely at Mom. Her eyes are a bit glazed. My stomach does a flip-flop. *Oh no. Not again.* I'm afraid to ask but I need to know.

"Are you on something?"

"What?" Mom brushes a lock of hair away from her eyes and refuses to meet my gaze. "No! Of course not. You know I don't do that anymore."

Mom had a problem with some drugs a year ago. That's how she lost her nursing job.

I nod. "Of course."

But something isn't sitting right with me. She's awfully perky, but in a fake sort of way. I won't bring up Cory tonight.

After dinner she puts frosting on the cake. I cut myself a big slice of cake and pour a glass of milk to wash it down.

"I'll clean up," she says. "You go and do homework."

I return to the living room with my cake, but I feel unsettled. A text pops in from Cory. I'm up to my eyeballs in homework! There's a little emoji of rolling eyes.

I laugh and reply: Me too! Then I stack my calc book on top of my English Lit book and text him a photo. I was about to Snap it but it occurs to me that I don't follow him on anything. I never even asked his last name.

He sends a smiley back. And he adds a heart.

I text a heart back to him and then open my Lit book.

After a while, Mom appears in the doorway. "I'm going to go take a shower," she says.

I wait until I hear the water running, and then I hurry into her bedroom. The bathroom door is closed and I can hear her in the shower, singing. I open her nightstand drawer and look under the carefully folded handkerchiefs. I mean, who uses handkerchiefs anymore? And there it is. An unmarked bottle of pills. I open them. Little white ones. These are the same ones she was using last year. She lost her nursing job then, but I'm sure she still has connections. I count them. There are nineteen.

Should I confront her? Should I tell Brit's mom? Or call our social worker?

I put them back where I found them and close the drawer. This is too much for me to deal with. I don't really have any proof she's taking them. Maybe she's just doing better. Maybe she's on an upswing.

But I don't really believe that.

Do I?

Cory texts again. Some medical humor: A patient tells his doctor "I get heartburn every time I eat birthday cake." The doctor replies: "Next time take off the candles first."

I laugh out loud and send him a smiley.

Mom is still singing in the shower. Softly. It's "Hey Jude" by the Beatles.

I think of what Brit said about Harvard, and I dial Cory's number before I lose my nerve.

He answers immediately. "Hey."

"Hey," I say. "Can you talk?"

"Yeah. Give me a minute."

There's some silence, and then his voice is back. "That's better. I was in the library studying with some guys from class, but now I'm out in the hallway. What's up?"

"Um...I was wondering..."

I stop. I don't want him to think this is the only reason I'm interested in him.

"Heather?" he says. "You can talk to me about anything, you know."

The way he says that makes me feel like he's really sincere. Like he wants to know me better and will like me no matter what. I take a deep breath. "I was wondering...when you go see your dad this weekend, can you ask him to talk to his friend about getting me into Harvard?"

I close my eyes and wait.

But Cory laughs. "Of course! I was planning on it!"

I open my eyes. "You were?"

"Yes!" he says. "I mean, why not? It's your dream, and it's obvious you're a hard worker. Maybe he can do something. Don't get your hopes up, but you never know."

"Thanks, Cory. This means a lot to me."

"I should get back to studying," he says.

"Okay."

"Heather?"

Mom turns off the water in the shower.

"What?" I say quietly into the phone.

"I'll miss you this weekend."

"I'll miss you too."

We hang up, and I hurry back to the living room. I feel a little hope stirring inside me about Harvard. I go into the kitchen to get a second piece of cake. It's delicious. I decide to enjoy my time with Mom tonight. I'll worry about her drug habit tomorrow.

Chapter 9

Cory heads back to New York on Friday, while I suffer through a boring day at school. By Saturday I am really missing him. I thought maybe he would text me, but I guess he's busy with family stuff.

I work most of the day at the café on Saturday. We're super busy. There's a craft show at the church next door, and people keep filing in afterwards with bags of hand-painted items. They sit in groups of friends and talk, and order lattes or lunches.

By Saturday evening, I'm exhausted. Mom is working late so I heat up yesterday's leftovers for us and have it ready by 7 p.m. when she gets home. She's wearing her uniform for Mark's Grocery, where she clerks.

"My feet are killing me," she says, taking her coat off and sitting down at the table. "Thanks so much for cooking!" Her eyes have that glazed look again.

After dinner she goes and props her feet up while I do the dishes. I'm debating on if I should ask her about the pills in her drawer. I decide not to.

When I go out into the living room, she's dozing in the chair. I sneak into her bedroom and quietly open her dresser drawer. I count the pills. There are sixteen today.

I put them back, not caring that I left them on top of the handkerchiefs instead of underneath.

"Heather?" Mom calls from the living room.

I wander back in. She's sitting up now, her feet off of the ottoman. "Do you want to play a game? I found Scrabble in the basement yesterday."

I look at my mom and remember how she used to be. Before.

"No," I say. "I have a lot of homework to do."

Without waiting for her to answer, I retreat to my room and close the door.

I sit on my bed. The green comforter reminds me of a forest. I wish I could get lost in it.

I decide to text Cory.

How is your trip going?

Awesome! He texts back. **Will tell you about it on Monday. GTG. Dad doesn't like phones at the table. ;-)**

That sounds so sweet and homey. I text back **Okay. C U later!**

Then I text Brit and make plans to go over to her house tomorrow.

Chapter 10

Brittney's family attends church. It's some Baptist church on the edge of town. I've been with her to youth group a few times, but my parents and I were never really church attenders. I prefer to sleep in.

So I go over after lunch.

Brittney has the perfect family. Her mom stays home and is available to drive Brittney and her brother around to all of their events. Her dad is an accountant, and he's super nice. He plays the guitar. When I get there, I hear him in the back room, strumming away on it. He's playing some folksy tune from the seventies that I recognize but don't know the name of.

"Have you had lunch?" Brit's mom asks me.

"Yes," I say. It was a microwave burrito. Not the best thing I've eaten all week.

Brittney and I are leafing through the latest sales catalogue from the store where Brit works. "I love this dress," Brit says, pointing at a lilac sheath. "Maybe I'll get it for prom. Do you think Aaron would like it?"

It's really pretty. And modest enough that her mom would probably allow it.

"I like it," I say, truthfully.

"How's your mom doing?" Brittney's mom asks me. She sets a bowl of baby carrots down in front of me and a small bowl of ranch dressing.

"She's doing really great," I lie. I dip a carrot in the dressing and take a bite. I smile up at Mrs. Roberts for maximum benefit. She smiles back.

Last year when Mom had to go into rehab for her drug habit, I moved in with the Roberts for two weeks. I thought it would be like a big sleepover with my best friend, but instead it felt weird. Like they were all watching me to be sure I was okay. And there's only one shower in their house, and we all had to volley for shower time and stuff. They were super nice to me, but I just wanted to be in my own home.

"She made this awesome dinner Thursday night and we still have some chocolate cake left over," I add.

Mrs. Roberts nods. "That's wonderful. I'm really glad to hear it."

If I tell the truth, she'll call the social worker and we'll start the whole thing over again. But Mom probably needs help. I feel a pang of guilt in my gut and decide to ignore it.

"Do you want to watch a movie?" Brit asks.

We find a chick-flick on Netflix. When it's over, we head into Brittney's bedroom to study for a while. She asks some questions about Cory and I answer what I can.

"You have it bad," she teases.

I think she's right. I think I'm falling in love.

Chapter 11

Monday morning during quiet work time in Chem, I get the email from the University of Michigan. "We regret to inform you...."

I close my email app without reading the rest. I feel tears prick my eyes and I fight them back. Brit, who is sitting next to me, notices.

"What?" she mouths.

I hand her my phone and let her read the email.

"Oh, Heather," she says, and looks like she's about to cry for me.

But I don't want her pity. I don't want anybody's pity. That was my last chance. I take my phone back and head up to Mr. Mitchell's desk to ask for a bathroom pass.

In the girls' bathroom, I close the door and let the tears come. Do you have any idea how hard it is to sob silently? But I do. And I blow my nose so much I use half the toilet paper role.

When I try to flush it down, the toilet clogs.

Great.

Instead of going back to class, I head to the guidance counselor.

"Heather!" she says cheerily. Mrs. Neilson is a morning person. But then she sees my face. "Uh-oh."

I plop ungracefully down in her chair. Her quote-of-the-day calendar reads "If you can dream it, you can do it."

"Michigan hates me," I said.

She folds her hands together and looks at me across her desk. "You didn't get in?"

I shake my head, feeling the tears threaten again. "Now what?"

"You still have plenty of great options," she says. She digs out my folder and opens it up. Then she starts to list the schools who have let me in. None of them are schools I want to go to.

"And you'll get aid since you only have one parent," she says.

Perfect. I get the dead-parent pity money from the schools. Is that supposed to be some sort of bonus to make up for having your dad die?

I don't listen as she drones on. Instead, I feel this pit of despair come over me. I wonder if I am going to be depressed like Mom. Maybe they can lock me up too. Then I won't have to do anything. I can rest.

After four years of working myself to death over grades, I can finally rest. They'll bring me meals and everything.

"I should get back to class," I say. Without waiting for her to respond or give me a pass, I get up and walk out.

I mope about all day and avoid Brit. After class I go home to change, and Mom isn't there. She's at work again. I go and count her pills. Four more are missing.

At work, I look for Mr. Sneeder. I need someone else to tell my college troubles to. But he isn't there. He hasn't been there in a few days. I wonder if he's sick.

That night at home I don't do any homework. I just crawl into bed, smelling like coffee. Gracie is laying on my bed, purring. I'm about to drift off to sleep when I get a text. It's from Cory.

Sorry I didn't call today. Crazy day! But I have some exciting news for you. I'll tell you tomorrow! And there's a heart emoji.

Tell me now! I text back.

Nope. I want to tell you in person. Good night!

I send him a heart emoji back. Could it be about Harvard? I feel the little trickle of hope return. But I don't want to get my hopes up. So, I pull the covers over my head and go to sleep.

Chapter 12

Today is an assembly honoring Women's History Month. It was planned long before last week's assembly on Yes Means Yes, so I guess the teachers feel the need to go ahead with it.

I don't know how we're supposed to get our academics done with all this stuff going on.

I see Brit up near the top of the bleachers in the gym, next to Aaron and Dennis. I make my way up.

"Hey," I say, sitting next to her.

"Hey," Brit says. "Why didn't you answer my texts last night?"

But the assembly starts, so I don't have to respond.

Principal Make-It-So gets up and welcomes us. Then the dance club performs some strange dance with twirling scarves. I have no idea what this has to do with Women in History, but they get their moment in the spotlight, and it gives me time to get some bubble gum off of Dennis.

Then we see this stupid film about women throughout history and how they were oppressed. We couldn't vote. We couldn't own land. Blah blah blah.

I know all of this. Then the film starts celebrating women who made a difference. Kaitlyn B. Anthony. Amelia Earhart. Sally Ride. Then there's a slide of Fe Del Mundo, the first woman to enter Harvard.

So women couldn't attend college either?

Suddenly I'm angry at all of the women throughout history. I mean, who was the first woman who decided she'd let men control everything? Who first said we couldn't vote? Or own land? Or go to college?

Why didn't the women all rise up and revolt eons ago? *Geez.*

Before I know what I'm doing, I get up to leave. Stupid women. Stupid assembly. All they had to do was fight back.

I hear Brittney call my name but the blood is roaring in my ears. I stomp down the bleachers and past one of my teachers sitting near the bottom. Ms. Marple looks up at me.

"Bathroom," I say before she can ask.

In the bathroom I let the water run as I stare at myself in the mirror.

Stupid women. Stupid me.

I think about all the hours I poured into studying. All the AP tests I took over the years, even though they were expensive. All the stress.

I think about the internship I did last summer at the clinic, so I could log in some medical hours. Between that and my job at the café, summer was pretty much full-time work.

And for what?

"Heather?"

I jump. It's Brittney.

"Are you okay?" she asks.

I shake my head no.

I think of the rejection emails, and of the little bottle of pills in my mom's drawer. Of her months of depression. Of the money I sometimes have to spend from my job to buy groceries.

Brittney waits for me to say more, but suddenly it's all too much. College. Mom and her drug problem. Our lack of money. There comes a point when, if you haven't kept your best friend up on what's going on in your life, it's too hard to explain.

"I'm fine," I say and shut the water off. "Let's get back." I brush past her and out into the hall. Fortunately for me, the bell is now ringing, and we have to go to class.

"Let's talk," Brittney says, following me. But I shake my head 'no' and blow her off.

Then after school, I tell her I need to go right to work and can she get a ride home with someone else? She does, and I leave for home.

— — —

At work I try to focus on my job, but I keep looking towards the door. Cory texted earlier that he'd be by around 7 p.m. I have butterflies in my stomach, because whatever he has to say will determine my future. My life.

I arrange to take my break then. Sure enough, about five minutes to seven, he walks in the door. I still can't get over how cute he is. He has that long lock of hair hanging over his left eye, and he gives me his shy grin and a small wave.

"He's here. I'm taking my break now," I tell Cherise, and untie my apron.

I go over to the table where Cory is standing. He's taking off his jacket, but he stops what he's doing to give me a quick kiss on the lips. I *know* Cherise saw that! I try to hold back the smile that is threatening to take over my face.

"I'm on break, so we can talk for a few minutes," I say, pulling out a chair and sitting.

"I missed you!" he says, taking a seat across from me. He reaches over the table and takes my hands in his.

"I missed you too," I say, because it's true. My stomach is swirling with either anxiety and excitement. I can't tell which. Maybe both.

"So…" he says, and smiles. "I'll bet I know what you're waiting to hear."

"Stop!" I say, because he's teasing me. But I laugh. I'm suddenly nervous. "So get on with it!"

"My dad talked to his friend about you, and he says there are always openings left over at Harvard, and always unclaimed scholarship money. He thinks he can help you out."

My heart starts pounding in my chest. This is the best news I've had in weeks. Months, even.

"Really?" I say, not quite believing it.

Cory nods.

"He wants to see your transcripts and college essay."

"Okay. I can print those out or email them—"

"Even better," Cory says, his eyes sparkling. "He wants to meet you in person."

"What?"

46

"Yes. That's what he says. I'm heading home again this weekend, and he said he'd love to interview you. *In person.*"

"So like…I'd go to Harvard *this weekend?*" I'm trying to figure out the logistics of this.

"Not exactly. He and my dad have been wanting to get together, so Dad invited him to dinner next Friday night at our house. Come home with me. I can drive. We can leave Friday morning, be there by dinner time. Saturday we can sightsee. I can have you back Sunday."

"Wow," I say. I think for a minute. It sounds too good to be true. "I mean…we've only known each other for a week…"

Cory sits back. "I know. And this isn't a way to get you… you know…to get alone with you. It's just to help you out. You can sleep in my sister's bedroom. She's away at college. And my dad will be there all weekend."

"Of course. It's all cool," I say. My head is spinning with the possibilities. *Harvard!* People say, it's *who* you know, not what you know. This is amazing!

For the rest of my shift, my mind is busy planning. I wish Daddy was here so I could tell him. If I can go to Harvard, I can start my medical studies. And Cory said they could get me scholarship money! I'm so happy I can barely focus. I accidentally put milk into a dairy-free latte and have to remake it.

When we close up, Cory walks me to my car. "I'd love to do dinner tonight, but I really need to get my nose back into my books," he says.

"That's okay. And thank you *so much* for talking to your dad."

"No problem," Cory says. He leans forward and kisses me. This kiss is longer than the other ones, and I can feel my tummy tingling with the anticipation of more. But I'm also a bit afraid to go further. I mean, he's a college guy, and I'm… well, he's my first real boyfriend. I'm sure he's plenty more experienced than I am with this sort of thing.

"I'll see you tomorrow?" he asks.

I nod and tell him to meet me at the city library. I'm not ready for Mom to meet him just yet.

— — —

I wait until lunch the next day to tell Brittney.

"What? Absolutely not!" Brit says right away.

"What do you mean? It's my chance to get into Harvard! *Harvard*, Brit!"

"You've only known this guy for a week."

"So? He's super sweet."

"Brit has a good head on her shoulders," Aaron says to my benefit.

"Thanks, A," I say.

"No prob."

Dennis is eating his sandwich. Pickles and cheese on Rye. He pushes his glasses up with his finger. "What does your mom think about this?" he asks.

"My mom?"

"She hasn't told her." Brit says matter-of-factly.

I sigh. Of course I haven't told my mom. She'd have a heart attack, and it would be a definite no.

"She hasn't told her mom she's going to go off to New York City with a college guy she just met?" Dennis says.

When I hear it said out loud, I can kind of see why they're worried.

"I want to meet him first," says Brit. Her arms are crossed and she has that look in her eye. "Then I can tell if he's safe."

"Doesn't your mom have that family app on your phone?" Aaron asks. "The one where she can track you? So you kind of have to tell her."

I hadn't thought of that. "Yes. She does."

"That's not a problem," says Dennis. "I can change your location."

"Dennis!" says Brittney. "You're not helping. Not one bit. We're supposed to be discouraging her. What does that even mean, you can 'change' it?" She does air quotes.

Yes. I'm wondering the same thing.

"I can change her location so that her GPS says she's at Brittney's house. Or wherever she wants to be. I do it all the time to play Pokémon Go. Sometimes there's a really cool one in Chicago, or someplace I can't actually *be*. I can catch a Downriver Pokémon while sitting in class."

"Cool!" Aaron says. "How do you do that?"

"With an app. And some savvy nerd knowledge."

But that's perfect. I can have him change my GPS location so it says I'm at Brittney's house. Then I'll tell Mom that I'm spending the weekend with her. We used to have sleepovers all the time when we were kids, and I still spend the night over there every now and then, so it's a great cover story.

"I don't want any part of this," Brittney says.

"Brittney, please," I say. "This is my only chance. Michigan rejected me."

"Oh, Heather…I mean, what if she calls?" Brit says. "I'm not lying for you."

"She won't call," I say. "I'll text her a bunch over the weekend. That will keep her happy."

The bell rings for class so Brittney has run out of time to argue. Dennis tells me to give him my phone at the end of the day tomorrow, and he'll change my location. Mom shouldn't stalk me on Friday. She'll be busy at work and assume I'm at school.

"You don't know this guy," Brittney says again. "I'm totally against this."

But I convince her not to say anything to my mom, by telling her I'll rethink the situation. Of course, I've already decided.

I'm going to New York.

Chapter 13

There ends up being no time for Brittney to meet Cory. He's super busy with school.

He picks me up Friday morning at 8 a.m. My mom is still sleeping. I sneak out of the house with my weekend bag, a printed copy of my resume and college essay carefully packed inside a folder. I also bring my school backpack, just in case. I should probably try to do some homework this weekend. I have a paper due in English on Monday.

I'm waiting outside when Cory pulls into the driveway, because I don't want to wake mom. Cory is dressed in blue jeans and a U of M sweatshirt. The top is up on his car because it's cold outside. When I get in, he leans over and kisses me on the lips.

"Good morning," he says.

"Good morning!"

He hands me a bag. "Bagels," he says.

I peek inside and pull out a cinnamon one. This is going to be so fun!

I called in sick to school this morning, then left my Mom a note on the kitchen table saying I would be at Brittney's after school. Later, I'll text her that we're doing a movie-marathon with ice cream, and that I'm spending the night.

On Saturday, I'll text her that I'm at work. But in reality, I'll call in sick. And then Saturday night I'll call her and say I'm back at Brit's because Mrs. Roberts has invited me to a belated birthday party dinner for Brit's brother.

I have it all planned out.

It's a ten-hour drive. Cory figures that will get us to his dad's house at about 6 p.m. Just in time for dinner. His dad's friend is coming over tonight, so I'll have my chance then to talk to him about Harvard. His name is Bram Stafford. It sounds very professorly. I'm a little bit nervous, but I'm also very excited.

That, Cory says, will get the school stuff out of the way so we can go sightseeing tomorrow. He says he can't wait to show me New York, a city he just loves.

"Your mom was okay with this?" Cory asks.

I hesitate. But this is Cory. I feel I can be honest with him. "She doesn't know. I told her I was going to Brittney's tonight."

"Can't she track your phone? My dad used to do that with me."

"No. My friend is a big computer geek. He changed my location so my GPS reads that I'm at Brittney's. She hardly ever checks, but if she does, it won't be until tonight."

"Oh." He gets quiet, as if thinking.

"It'll be okay," I say, hoping he's not upset.

"I know. I just like honesty, is all." But he lets it go and asks about what other schools I applied to.

We talk for a while about college, and then we focus on the music. He has a great playlist on his phone, which he pumps out through the Bose speakers in his car.

We stop briefly for lunch at a sub shop, but he insists we eat on the road. "Otherwise we won't make it in time," he says. I'm very careful not to spill on his leather seats.

We are quiet for a while, each of us busy eating. When he's finished he asks about Brit.

"How did you two meet?" he asks, sucking the last sip of his pop through his straw.

I tell him, and then add in some crazy stories from when we were younger. He tells me some funny things about his college roommates and we laugh a lot. I find out that he loves ice cream, the color blue, and wants to learn to play the guitar. It also turns out we have some favorite movies in common. The nervousness I felt earlier about going away with him is gone, and I feel so content and comfortable sitting beside him now.

Later in the afternoon, I offer to help drive, but he says he's fine. I drift off to sleep.

When I wake up, we're in New York.

"We're almost there," he says.

I look out the window at the large expanse of the city. The tops of the tallest skyscrapers disappear in a dense cloud of grey fog. Or smog. It's not a very pretty day. I wonder what it looks like when the sun is shining.

"My dad is on the outskirts of the city," says Cory. "But we can take the subway in tomorrow. It's so expensive to park."

He gets off the freeway and makes a few turns, driving for about fifteen more minutes. Then he pulls into a subdivision with big houses. Most of them sit on at least an acre of land, surrounded by trees for privacy. You can't even tell you're in a sub.

"Wow," I say.

He pulls into the circular driveway of a big, brick mansion. There's a fountain in the middle of the circle, but it's turned off for winter. It's the Greek god Poseidon (which I know from English class, thank you Mrs. Welch from ninth grade!). The god has his trident raised. I'll bet it's beautiful in the summer.

Cory stops on the driveway, just below the front door. Looking through the car window, I count the steps leading up to the double doors. There are exactly thirteen. Two pots sit on either side of the door, containing some type of pruned evergreen bush.

"This is your *home?* What does your dad do again?"

Cory laughs. "This is where I grew up," he says. "Dad is in real estate."

He turns the car off and gets out.

"I'll come around and help you with your bags," he says.

He opens the front door and lets me go in ahead of him.

The house is huge. Straight ahead is a big room that looks like a living room. On either side of us is a big, winding staircase going up to the second floor from the foyer, and high above me is a crystal chandelier. We set our bags down by the door, and Cory motions for me to follow him through into the living room.

"Welcome!" A tall, dark-haired man walks over to me, his arms spread wide. He's carrying a basket in his right hand. "You must be Heather," he says. "Cory has told me so much about you!" He gives me a little hug. "I'm his dad. You can call me Roger."

"Hi," I say. There's a wonderful smell coming from the kitchen area, and I realize how hungry I am.

"The roast is almost ready. Why don't you go dress for dinner?" Roger says to Cory.

Roger holds out the basket. "We have a no-screen-time rule at dinner," he says to me. "I need your phone please."

"My phone?"

But Cory takes his out of his pocket and drops it in the basket. "One of Dad's rules," he says. "He calls this family time."

Roger laughs, and I hand him my phone. That's kind of cool, I guess. Brit's parents don't allow phones at the table either.

Roger takes the basket with our phones in it and retreats into another room, which I assume is the kitchen.

"Dress for dinner? Like…how dressy?" I whisper to Cory, looking down at the jeans I'm wearing. I brought some nice slacks and a business-like top, but no dress.

"I'll show you my sister's room," he says. "She's away at college. You can wear something of hers. You look about the same size."

"I can't wear her clothes!" I say, but Cory has picked up my bags and is leading me upstairs.

"I'm sorry," he apologizes. "I should have told you. What did you bring?"

"Just some dress clothes, more business-like. That's what I thought I'd wear tonight for dinner."

"Dad likes formal."

Cory's sister's room is enormous and has a queen-size bed against one wall. The colors are dark crimson and light rose. Very pretty.

He leads me over to the closet. "Take your pick," he says. It's a walk-in. "I'll wait downstairs." He gives me a kiss and leaves.

There are three formal-length dresses in the huge closet, along with several different pairs of shoes. Along the back of the closet is a full-length mirror. This place is amazing!

It feels kind of weird to look at someone else's clothes. I wonder if she'll mind. But I take the yellow dress off the rack and hold it up to me. It's beautiful, with a cream-colored sash coming down across the shoulder and around the waist. I love it, but I wonder if yellow makes me look too young. There's a red dress and a dark blue dress. I pull out the dark blue. It goes well with my dark hair, so I try it on. It fits perfectly. It's a little low cut, but I think I look pretty awesome in it.

Then I check the shoes. There's a blue pair of heels that are a size seven and a half. I wear an eight, but my toes can suffer tonight. I put them on and love the look. I wish Brit could see me. I'm about to Snap her a photo when I realize I don't have my phone.

There's a private bathroom right inside the bedroom. I can't even imagine living like this! My entire house could almost fit into this bedroom. Well, not exactly, but *almost*. I riffle through my purse and pull out what I need to freshen up my makeup. Then I brush out my hair. I have a ponytail holder, and I put my hair into an updo. I pull a few strands loose to hang around my ears and soften up my look. Brit and I have spent years playing with our hair. I have some pretty good styles figured out, and this is one of my favorites.

I don't look like a high-school kid anymore. I look like a college girl.

I'm so happy I could burst.

Then, I remember why I'm really here. I dig into my bag and pull out the folder with my printed college essay, resume and transcripts in it. I tuck it under my arm.

My future is about to begin!

Chapter 14

As I walk down the winding staircase, I pretend I'm a princess descending for the royal ball. Brittney would love this! I'm about to text her when I remember again that I don't have my phone. I'll have to tell her all about this place tonight. I'm so glad I came!

At the foot of the stairs I turn right and walk into the living room. I hear voices coming from a room to the left of that. I follow them and discover a formal dining room. There are huge windows with tall red velvet drapes hanging from ceiling to floor. The furniture looks antique.

Cory and his dad are seated at a big oval table with three other men. They are laughing and joking. As soon as they see me, Cory stands. He's dressed in a dark blue suit with a creamy satin shirt underneath. He looks amazing.

He pulls a chair out for me.

"Wow," he says, and his eyes sparkle as he notices my dress and hair.

"You too," I say quietly, so only he can hear. He looks incredibly handsome, and I notice we are both wearing blue. How romantic!

I sit down and Cory sits down next to me. I put the folder on the table next to me and suddenly realize that it has frayed edges. And one of the corners must have gotten bent in my bag. I cover that corner with my napkin.

"Heather! You look beautiful!" Roger says from his place at the head of the table. "Let me introduce you. This is my friend from college, Bram Stafford."

Bram, who is sitting across from me, nods his head. His eyes sparkle. His hair is grayer than Cory's dad's, which makes him look older. I notice he has a little bit of a gut. He looks very much like a professor.

Roger motions to the other two men. "And these gentlemen are John and Christopher."

Both men nod.

"I'll check the food," Roger says, getting up and going into the kitchen.

While he's gone, a thin girl walks into the room and slides into the chair next to John. She looks younger than me but is all dressed up in a low cut red dress and has makeup on that makes it hard to guess her age. She's wearing her wispy, blond hair down over her shoulders. She keeps her eyes on her plate.

"It's ready!" Roger says, coming into the room with a platter. He sets it down in the middle of the table. It's a big pot roast, surrounded by tiny potatoes. There are already other sides on the table. A salad, fresh bread, some shrimp cocktail, and some type of green beans marinated in a buttery sauce.

I look up from the table and notice there's a redheaded girl now sitting next to the man named Christopher. I wonder when she came in. She's wearing a green dress and looks tired. Nobody bothers to introduce either of the girls. I wonder who the men are and if the girls are sisters or cousins or just friends. It seems a little odd. I'm about to ask Cory when Roger stands up.

"Welcome, friends," he says. "A toast!"

I notice there is wine in my glass. I'm not sure what to do. I glance at the other two girls, and they take their wine glasses unenthusiastically in their hands and raise them to Roger. Everybody is waiting for me. I pick mine up.

"A toast to good friends and a little bit of fun!" Roger says and laughs. The other men laugh too. Cory takes a swig of his wine.

I take a small sip. It burns going down. Some of the kids at school drink, and I had a half can of beer once at a party, but I've never had wine.

"And a toast to Heather," says Cory, lifting his glass to me. I lift mine again and we clank them together.

"Hear, hear!" says Roger, and we all take another drink.

The food is passed around the table. Roger starts to talk about his hunting escapades as he carves the roast and gives everybody a slice. Then John goes on about his computer business.

The men are busily eating, wiping the juices off of their chins. I wonder when we'll get around to talking about Harvard. I want to ask Bram some questions. Maybe I should just speak up.

I glance at the girls, who are both picking at their meals. I wonder why. The food is delicious. Neither of them has spoken.

I look over at Cory. He seems relaxed but notices me looking at him.

"I think he wants to talk to you after dinner," Cory whispers into my ear.

I nod to let him know I understand. The movement makes me a little dizzy. It's hot in here. I look for some water, but there is none. I take another small sip of wine.

The men keep eating. They're talking about something else now. I realize my plate is nearly empty. I don't remember eating all of that. I look across the table at Bram, who wipes his mouth and puts his napkin down.

Roger brings them another round of beer.

Bram takes a swig of his beer. I notice the blonde-haired girl is gone, and so is John. Then I see the redhead get up and leave the room. Christopher follows her, taking his beer with him. They leave the room and head towards the stairs.

"So Heather, you have something you want to show Bram, right?" Cory says.

"Oh, yes," I say, straightening up in my chair. Now's my chance. I reach for the folder, but it's not there. Where did it go?

"I think you left it in your room," Cory says. "Why don't you go and get it?"

I could have sworn I brought it down. "Okay." I stand and feel a little wobbly. What's wrong with me? Apparently I can't handle even a little wine. I'm drunk. I feel like a fool.

"Don't be nervous," Cory says quietly. He gives my hand a brief squeeze.

I nod and make my way over to the stairs. I climb them, and when I'm in my room, it takes me a minute to remember what I came for.

The folder.

The curtains have been drawn, and it's dark in here. I turn on the light switch, which illuminates a dim lamp on a dresser. I see my bag in the corner and I walk over to it. Maybe I left it in there.

"Lose something?"

I turn. It's Bram. He has followed me upstairs.

"I was just looking for…"

I notice he has closed the door behind him. He locks it.

"I know what you have for me," Bram says. His voice has a deep, suggestive quality, and he is grinning. He reminds me of a wolf. He crosses the room until he's standing in front of me.

"I want to go to Harvard," I say. I blurt the words out because suddenly I'm scared. This is all so wrong. Why is he upstairs in the bedroom with me? Why did he lock the door? My heart starts pounding.

"Do you want to show me how much you appreciate me?" he asks. "Maybe some incentives from you will help me with my decision." He puts his hand on my cheek and leans down to kiss me on the lips.

I freeze. Does he expect me to have sex with him in order to get into Harvard? His lips are dry and feel chapped.

I pull away from him. "Cory." I try to scream for him, but my voice doesn't seem to be working. It comes out a quiet whisper.

I'm scared.

Bram reaches behind me and unzips my dress. It falls to the ground, and suddenly I'm standing there in just my underwear.

He presses himself against me until I fall backwards onto the bed.

"No," I say weakly, but I can't seem to stop him. My muscles aren't cooperating.

He lays on top of me and unhooks my bra. I try to push him away, but my arms are pinned under his weight. And I am so weak. Then I feel him reach and pull my underwear down.

I am totally naked now, and the bed comforter is cold against my back. Part of my brain wonders why he didn't turn down the comforter to get to the sheets. None of this makes sense.

I try to raise my head but the room is spinning.

"Stop," I say. "I haven't done this before. Please stop."

"I know you haven't done this before," he says into my neck as he's kissing me. His stubble of a beard is burning my skin. "I paid extra for a virgin."

Paid?

Where's Cory? Why isn't he here helping me? Why hasn't anybody come to check on me? I'm in a panic as I try to scream Cory's name again, and this time my voice comes out, and it sounds loud. I scream again and Bram, or whatever his name is, quiets me by smashing his lips against mine. He tastes of beer and onions.

I realize I am crying, and I try to push him off, but he's heavy, and my arms are weak. My muscles don't seem to be working right. The room won't quit spinning.

I am helpless to stop him. I feel pain between my legs, a *lot* of pain, and I am crying. His body is pumping against mine, rocking the entire bed.

"Please stop," I say through tears, but he pushes his lips against mine again, and I can barely breathe.

Then, after what seems like forever, he rolls over and lays beside me. I realize now is my time to escape, but my arms are too heavy to work, and I can't seem to move my legs. I try to lift my head, and everything fades to black.

— — —

When I wake up, I am naked and cold. I'm also alone. I try sitting up, but that makes my head pound, so I lay back down.

My thighs are wet, and when I reach down and pull my hand back, it is sticky and bloody.

I roll over onto my side and curl up in a ball. I pull the corner of the comforter up over me. And I cry some more until I drift off to sleep.

— — —

The next time I wake up my head feels better. There's some light coming in from around the curtains. Is it morning? I sit up and panic, looking for my clothes. I feel gross and stagger naked into the bathroom. I'll take a shower. No, I need to leave. My head is still thick with confusion.

I turn and go back into the bedroom and see my underwear laying on the carpet near the bed. My dress is crumpled up on the floor a few feet from it.

What happened?

I try hard to remember. Professor Bram...he...

I suddenly feel nauseated and run back into the bathroom, where I throw up in the toilet. My stomach empties itself of everything until I only have dry heaves. It's hard to throw up and cry at the same time. After a few minutes, I close the lid and sit down, tears in my eyes. I am shaking.

Panic sets in as I try to figure out what to do next. Where's Cory? I need to find Cory. But then a weird sense of shame creeps in. He can't see me this way.

I let myself get drunk, and then I let Bram...

I stop the thought. I find a washcloth and wipe myself off, then hurry into the bedroom to look for my bag. It's in the corner, and I pull on some fresh underwear, a bra, and the jeans and t-shirt I had on when I arrived.

I need to find Cory. I need to find my phone.

But there's a nagging question chasing me—why didn't Cory come and check on me last night?

The room is dark from the heavy curtains, and the only light is coming from a small nightlight. My heart is pounding as I turn the door handle and peek out into the hallway. I don't see anyone, and I smell something cooking downstairs. There is light coming in through the downstairs windows. So it really must be morning. I was passed out all night.

I go down into the dining room, where I see Cory sitting at the table sipping coffee. Suddenly I'm afraid of him. I should have looked for another door. I never should have let them see me.

"There you are!" he says, calmly. "You never came back down last night. How'd it go?"

I don't know how to answer. I want to tell him I was raped. But I suddenly feel ashamed. And scared to tell him. What if he was part of it? What if he *knew?* But no. Not Cory. And if he doesn't know, what will he think if he knows I had sex with Bram?

I was so stupid to let myself get drunk.

"Where's my phone?" I say.

"Dad has it," he says, standing up, a look of concern coming into his eyes. "What's wrong?"

I bite my lip but the tears come into my eyes anyway. "I want to go home."

"Heather?" Cory says, and walks towards me. He reaches out to take my hand but I back away.

His dad suddenly comes into the room. "Good morning, Heather!" he says. He's all chipper. Here's an adult who can help me. Right? Isn't that what adults do? Or is he in on this too? He has to be. It has to be him. Or what if neither of them knew? What if they thought Bram was helping me with college last night?

But *upstairs?* In the sister's *bedroom?*

"I—" I start to speak. But I'm too embarrassed to tell him. I was *drunk*. What if it's *my* fault?

"I need my phone," I say.

"I forgot to plug it in last night," Roger says. "It's charging."

"I need it."

I look wildly around the room for a land line. I can call 911. But what will I tell them? That's when I see the blond-haired girl from last night. She's sleeping on the couch and our voices don't seem to have awakened her.

"Have some breakfast," Cory says. He slides a basket of bagels across the table towards me.

I feel nauseated.

"What's wrong?" Cory asks again.

"I have a headache."

He pulls a plastic baggie of pills out of his pocket. "Aspirin. Take one of these. It'll help."

I shake my head no. Why does he have pills in a baggie?

I still haven't sat. Cory and his dad are both looking at me.

"I don't feel so well," I say. Why aren't they more concerned that I never came back down last night? Where is Bram? I look around the room, new fear going through me, but he's nowhere in sight.

"Sit down, Heather," Roger says.

I shake my head and move toward the front door. Suddenly Roger has his hand on my arm. I feel a shot of adrenaline at his touch and I try to pull away, but he holds on tight. He turns me around and looks closely at my eyes.

"Oh *no*," he says, shaking his head. "You were given some DHG in your wine last night," he says, and leads me back over to the table. His hand is digging into my arm. "Bram must have slipped it in. I don't know what happened, but we need to get you to the hospital. And then I'll call the police. Did..." He looks at me. "Did anything happen?"

I nod as tears spill out of my eyes. Finally someone is taking charge. He is figuring it all out. What is DHG? Does Bram often do this to girls? If so, why did Roger leave me alone with that man? Roger pulls two pills out of the baggie Cory put on the table.

"Pour her some orange juice," he says to Cory. I look at Cory, who pours some juice from a pitcher into a glass and brings it to me.

"Take these," his dad says. "It's aspirin. It'll help clear your head. Then drink some juice, and we'll get you to the hospital."

I don't want to go to the hospital. I want to go home. But I nod my head and swallow the pills.

"I need to call my mom," I say.

"Of course," says Roger. "I'll go get your phone."

Cory comes over and puts his arm around me, as Roger leaves. His arm feels warm and comforting. He didn't know. How could he? He pulls out a chair for me and I sit. I'm very sore.

"Heather?" Cory says again. "What happened?"

I feel a flash of anger. Is he *serious?* How stupid is he? "*Why* didn't you come looking for me last night?" I ask.

"Tell me what happened," he says.

"Here," Roger hands me my phone. I turn it on. There's no signal. No internet.

"The Internet must be down," says Roger. "We don't usually get a signal in here. Cory, go downstairs and check the connection."

My panic returns. I suddenly don't want Cory to leave me. I want him to protect me from... Or did he bring me to this? Who can I trust?

The girl on the couch moans and turns over.

Cory is only gone for a few minutes. There's still no signal or internet connection. He takes my phone, and he and his dad look at it.

"Do you have a land line?" I say.

"No." Roger shakes his head. He looks at his own phone and swears. "No signal."

I'm so tired. It must be the left-over effects of the drug. DHG? Is that what they called it? I remember hearing that name someplace before. I try to think where, but my head really hurts, and things are still foggy.

"Let's get her to the hospital," Roger says.

"We need to call the police," I hear myself say.

"I will," Roger says. "But you need medical attention first. This drug can affect your heart. It can be fatal."

"Come on," Cory says. "We'd better get you checked out." He comes over and helps me stand. I feel a bit shaky. He puts his arm around me to support me. But he doesn't seem worried enough. If this were Aaron or Dennis, they'd be acting like first responders right now. And Brit? If Brit was here—

"Dad, will you get her coat?"

Roger leaves the room and returns with my coat. He helps me into it.

"My things..." I start to say, but Cory interrupts me.

"We'll come back for them. You don't look too good. Let's get you checked out."

I stop at the front door long enough to put my shoes on, and then Cory walks me out to his car. As he pulls out of the driveway, I feel so sleepy. I think I'll close my eyes for a few minutes.

63

Chapter 15

When I wake up, Cory's car is speeding down the highway. My head feels groggy. I need to call Brit. Or my mom. Or somebody. I reach into my coat pocket, but my phone isn't there. Where's my phone? I look around for my purse but then remember I left it in the bedroom. The hospital will want my insurance information. I don't have my wallet.

"I need my phone," I say.

"Who are you going to call?" Cory asks.

I think about that for a moment. Who *was* I going to call? Maybe my guidance counselor? Mrs. Neilson? What was I going to tell her? Oh yeah. That I'm not getting into Harvard.

I try to talk, but my tongue won't work. I don't think that was aspirin that Roger gave me. I feel a tightening in my chest, panic returning, but I can't muster up the energy to really panic. It's almost as if I am looking at myself through a lens. I can see myself sitting here, but I can't *feel* anything. I lean my head back against the headrest.

And I sleep.

Until I feel hands on me, dragging me out of the car. I moan. I want to keep sleeping.

The bitter wind bites through my jeans and wakes me up a little bit. But then I'm suddenly sitting in a chair in a living room. This isn't the hospital. Am I back at Cory's?

No.

I sit there for a few minutes, letting my head clear. The room is small, and the carpeting is dark green and dingy. There are scuff marks on the walls, and the faded armchair I'm sitting in is ripping out at the seams. I pick at a loose thread on the arm.

Then I hear voices. Cory is standing next to the front door talking with another man. He has short dark hair and stubble on his face. The man is older than Cory, maybe about thirty. He's thanking Cory.

"No problem, Tommy," Cory says. The man called Tommy hands Cory a wad of cash, and I watch as Cory counts it.

Cory looks like he's about to leave. I'm suddenly very scared. I don't want to stay here alone! I try to stand, but my legs are weak, and I have to sit back down. "Cory!" I say. He'll help me. He promised he would help me. That's why we came on this trip. So he could help me.

"Cory!" I say again. My voice is getting stronger. I'm waking up. He is supposed to take me to the hospital. His dad is supposed to call the police. This time I manage to stand.

Cory walks over to me and looks me in the eyes. "I'm sorry," he says. "You seem like a nice girl." He hands me the baggie of white pills. "Here. These will help you relax."

He starts to walk away, and I grab his arm. "Cory! What's happening? Where are we?"

I glance at the man called Tommy. He's of average size, maybe just under six feet. He's not as tall as Aaron. He's Caucasian, with brown eyes, and a tattoo of a naked woman on his left bicep. There's a snake entwined around her. His brown eyes meet mine and I don't like what I see.

"Cory!" I say. "Take me with you! I'm scared!" Part of me realizes Cory is the reason I'm in this place. But I know him. He'll have to help me. He's all I have at the moment.

He pulls my arm off of him.

"Goodbye, Heather," he says.

I scramble towards him on my wobbly legs, reaching out for him, trying to grab his arm again, frustrated that my body won't respond. But he's out the door before I get there. And then he's gone.

Chapter 16

Tommy closes the door and locks it. Then his eyes travel up and down me, as if he's measuring me.

A slow grin spreads across his face.

"Follow me," he says.

But I make a grab for the door handle. Quickly, his hand is on my wrist pulling me away. Then another man steps out of the hallway and plants himself between me and the front door.

"That's a no-no," Tommy says, wagging his finger at my face. "Come on. I'll introduce you to the others."

He leads me through a kitchen and into another room that has a television in it. It's not a fancy flat-screen. It's an old tube TV like my grandma used to own. There are some girls watching a show about tigers. I see a large tiger, a Bengal maybe, chasing down an antelope. I watch in horror as the big cat jumps on it and takes it to the ground. As the antelope struggles, the cat tears into its hindquarters with its jaws and rips off a piece. None of the girls seem startled by the violence.

There are three girls. They look about my age. Maybe younger. Maybe older. It's hard to tell. Two are smoking something that doesn't look like a regular cigarette. One is passed out asleep on the couch.

"This is Serena and Chloe," says Tommy, pointing to the two smoking girls. "And this here is Reg." Reg is the one who is passed out.

I don't understand what's going on. Why am I here? This looks like a hangout for drug addicts.

"I don't get it," I hear myself say.

"You work for me now," Tommy says. "This is your new home."

"My what?"

"You do as I say, and I will take care of you. If you don't do as I say…" he looks at the other girls. None of them meet his eyes. "Well, you'd just best play it safe and listen."

He glances at his watch. "It's time to go to work."

He grabs my wrist and yanks me towards the front door. I brace myself to run as soon as he opens it. But he has too tight of a hold on me.

As soon as we're outside, I scream. Tommy doesn't seem to care. I kick at his shins, his balls, any target I can find, but the white pills Roger gave me make me clumsy. Tommy sidesteps my efforts. I try to break loose, but he has a good grip. I kick out at him again, but my legs are still very weak, and they buckle. He pushes me in the backseat of the car and shuts the door.

I grab the handle, but it's locked from the outside somehow. Maybe child safety locks? Then another man slides in next to me from the other side. It's the thug I saw in the house.

"Going somewhere, sweetheart?" he asks.

I'm trapped. I look around.

We're in an old, rundown part of a town that I don't recognize. Windows are boarded up in many of the houses. Across the street, a few of the homes are burned down, leaving charred remains between barely-functioning homes.

Tommy gets in and starts driving. In just a few minutes, we arrive at a hotel. It's old and run down like the houses and has a neon sign that reads "vacancy." We don't go to the front desk. Instead, he pulls around back. All of the doors face the parking lot. The paint is peeling off of most of them.

The man next to me opens his car door and pulls me out. Tommy grabs my wrist and drags me to one of the hotel room doors and opens it. He pushes me inside and follows me in.

"You stay here," he says. "I'll be standing outside watching this door. If you try to leave, I will kill you." He pulls his shirt aside to reveal a knife. "You got it?"

I swallow hard and nod. "Please," I say. "I don't understand."

Tommy doesn't answer. Instead, he says, "A friend of mine will visit you soon. You show him a good time, or I'll kill you. Do you understand?"

I nod, but I don't understand. Why am I here?

Tommy turns and leaves, shutting the hotel door behind him. Suddenly I'm alone.

I look around for a way out, but there are no windows. And Tommy is standing outside my door

I look for a phone, but there is none. How can a hotel not have a phone?

Suddenly, there's a brief knock on the door. Then a man comes in and shuts it behind him. He locks it. He's big. Wearing jeans and a flannel shirt.

"You're mighty pretty," he says.

I back up towards the bed. I'm suddenly remembering parts of last night. Professor Bram walking towards me. Pushing me down on the bed.

Hurting me.

I'm starting to understand what's about to happen.

"I don't want to do this," I say, but my voice is barely a whimper.

The man doesn't seem to care what I want. He comes closer and puts his hand on my shoulder and leans in for a kiss. "You smell nice," he says. I think of Tommy standing outside with his knife.

The man pulls back a little and looks at me. He reaches his hand up and touches my cheek, runs his hand through my hair. "Shall we get started?"

I slap him across the face. It's not hard— my muscles are too weak right now. But it surprises him. He growls and hits me across the face with the back of his hand. My head snaps to the side, and I feel the burn on my cheeks. Black spots swim in front of my vision, and for a moment I have to fight to remain conscious.

The man hits me again. This time across the other cheek.

"Stop!" I say, and I aim a good kick at his crotch. I miss and kick his knee instead. He howls again and pushes me so hard I tumble backwards across the floor and slam against the far wall.

68

"What's all the commotion?" It's Tommy's voice. He has opened the door and is standing just inside it.

"Your girl here—" says the man.

Tommy nods and asks the man to step outside. Maybe he's going to help me. Maybe Tommy will see how he has hit me.

Instead, Tommy crosses the floor quickly until he's right up in my face He takes my chin in his left hand and squeezes. "You behave," he says. "Because I can do a lot worse to you than my client here." He lets go of my chin and grabs my shoulder, throwing me to the floor. I hit hard and my jeans tear in the knee, skinning my knee in the process.

Tommy crosses the floor and kicks me in the ribs. The air gushes out of me, and I bend over in pain. I'm sitting there, gasping for breath.

"Are you ready to behave?"

I nod. Because I don't have any choice. Not now. I'll have to wait until later to escape.

"Good," Tommy says. "Now stand up." He grabs my wrist and jerks me to my feet.

I stand, holding my stomach where he kicked me. He opens the door and lets the man back in. Then he leaves me alone with him.

Plaid-shirt guy grins again. "So you're a fighter, huh? Makes it all the more exciting."

— — —

When he leaves, I lay there, trembling. I'm also crying, I realize.

It doesn't seem like the man has been gone long when another man comes in.

I sit up and scoot back on the bed, cowering. "No," I say. But he doesn't listen to me either. I put up a fight again, kicking and screaming, but this only seems to make him laugh. He pins my wrists down.

I'm beginning to realize where I am. I'm in Hell.

— — —

After he's gone, Tommy comes in.

"You okay?" Tommy asks.

I'm not. I can't even speak.

He tosses the plastic baggie of pills at me. "Take one of these. It will help you relax." He looks on the dresser where there is some crumpled up money. He counts it, nods, and leaves.

The baggie of pills is sitting on the bed next to me. I remember my mom and the unmarked bottle of pills in her dresser. She takes them and feels better.

But I don't want to feel like I felt last night. The room spinning.

Then I remember that Cory gave me something like these this morning that made me sleepy. Maybe that's all these will do. Maybe I will just go to sleep, and when I wake up, I'll be home.

Mom's pills make her happy. The "I don't care" pills are what she called them when we were in therapy. She takes them and doesn't care. That's how she survives without my dad.

Maybe that's what these are. "I don't care" pills.

I reach for the baggie and notice that my hand is shaking. I hear male voices outside the hotel door. Tommy and somebody else.

I open the baggie and take one out and look at it. It looks harmless enough.

The door handle starts to turn. I panic and pull the covers up around me. But whoever is on the outside pauses.

I wait, holding the pill between the thumb and index finger of my left hand. I'm watching the door, listening to the male voices outside. Someone laughs.

The handle of the door turns some more, and another man walks through. He grins.

I swallow the pill without water.

Chapter 17

When Brittney turned thirteen, her dad took her out on a "date." They went to a restaurant and sat at a little booth in the back. He told her how much he loved her. She said he seemed really nervous.

Then he told her that she was special and that any man she dated should treat her with respect.

She said that he gave her a little gold heart necklace and fastened it around her neck with trembling fingers. The heart symbolized her love, and her dad had a tiny key made. When she found the man she wanted to marry, she could give him the key to her "heart."

The idea was that she remain a virgin until she got married. The Hudsons are conservative like that.

Brit and I laughed about it later, but she loved that necklace and still wears it every day. I never asked her what Aaron thought about it. But as far as I know, she's still a virgin. And I would know if she wasn't. Brit and I tell each other *everything*.

I remember the Monday after her birthday, when she came to school wearing that necklace. She brought in vanilla cupcakes with confetti frosting to share with our middle school home room. At lunch, she told me about the necklace and what it meant. I was a little bit jealous that I didn't have a dad to care so much about me.

Now, as I lay here alone, thinking of how many men I've been with in a single day, I touch my neck where there is no necklace. If *my* dad were alive and had given me a heart-shaped necklace with a key, he'd be very disappointed in me now.

It seems like I could have fought harder. Or done something to escape. Or maybe let them kill me instead.

I turn over and look at the clock. It's 3 a.m. It turns out that those little white pills in the baggie *are* the "I don't care" pills after all. Because the door handle is turning again, and I feel pretty numb about it all.

It's Tommy. He comes over and gathers the wad of money on the dresser.

"Get dressed, and let's go home," he says.

He tosses my clothes to me and watches as I put them on. Then he opens the door and follows me out. Part of my mind thinks of screaming for help, but who would come? I don't see anyone, and Tommy has his hand on my wrist. And maybe I shouldn't have taken that last pill.

He puts me in the backseat of the car and closes the door. And he drives. The landmarks are a blur in the darkness, and I'm having trouble staying awake. Soon, we're back at the house I left from earlier today, which seems like years ago.

He leads me into the kitchen and sits me down in one of the chairs. He pulls something out of the freezer and puts it in the microwave. In a minute or two, he sets it in front of me, along with a bottle of water. It's a burrito.

I'm starved. It has been a very long time since I last ate. I feel like I should be crying and fighting and trying to run, but much to my dismay I inhale the burrito instead.

Tommy smiles. "Looks like you worked up an appetite," he says.

I want to kill him.

When I finish the bottle of water, he takes my wrist and leads me to a back bedroom lit by a small desk lamp. There are two twin beds crammed into the small room. The passed-out girl I saw earlier, Reg, is sitting on one, reclined up against its headboard. She's smoking something that's smelling up the room. It makes me cough.

"This is where you sleep," Tommy says. "There's a bathroom down the hall on the right. There are men standing guard outside the house. Don't try to leave."

He retreats towards the bedroom door and then turns back. "Get some sleep, Heather. Tomorrow we will go over the rules."

Then he goes. He shuts the door behind him.

I glance at Reg and then make my way to the empty bed. I sit down, realizing I don't have my things. I don't have *any*thing. I wonder what I'm going to sleep in.

Reg is watching me through half-closed eyes. She takes another long drag of her joint. "In there." She nods towards a closet.

There's no door on it. There are clothes piled on three shelves, and a rack full of dresses and slips next to those.

I walk to the closet and find a pair of my underwear tossed on a shelf, with a few of the other clothes I brought with me to Cory's. I wonder how they got here, but I don't ask Reg. Instead, I change into clean underwear and pull on one of my t-shirts.

I'm cold, so I walk back to the bed and crawl under the thin blanket. I'm shaking.

Reg is still watching me. She has short-cropped black hair and is thin. Several piercings in her right eyebrow and ears catch the light. She's wearing a light blue t-shirt. Her long, bare legs stretch out across the bed, and there's a tattoo of a heart on her right leg.

"How old are you?" she asks.

"Seventeen."

Reg nods. "This your first day?"

It's my turn to nod. My first day of *what?* I feel tears starting. "Do you have a cell phone?" I ask.

Reg laughs. "You won't see one of those again." She leans over and holds out her joint. There are long scars up her bare arms. "Want a drag?"

I shake my head.

"Suit yourself," Reg says and leans back against her headboard. I don't know if it's the trauma or the pills I took, but I'm asleep in minutes.

— — —

I wake in a panic. There's sunlight streaming in through a bedroom window that I didn't notice was there last night. I sit upright, ignoring my full bladder. I have to get out of here.

Reg is still sleeping. I quietly pull on my jeans and push back the curtains from the window. There are bars on it. I grab them and shake but they don't move.

Outside is an empty backyard with a wooden fence around it. Dead weeds stand like sentinels across the frozen lawn, and some new green grass peeks up through the ground in places. The snow is almost all melted.

I'm running my hand along the window sill, looking for a lock, when my bedroom door opens.

"Going somewhere?" It's Tommy.

Fear grips my stomach, and I quickly shake my head.

"Breakfast," he says and walks back towards the kitchen. I follow him out but turn to use the bathroom.

After peeing, I wash my hands, and that's when I see myself in the mirror. I'm shocked at how terrible I look. Streaks of mascara and tears cover my face. I have a black eye. There are some paper towels on the counter, and I take one and wet it. I wipe my eye gently, because it's sore. I wash up the best I can, wiping the grime and foulness off of me from all of the men.

When I think of the men, my stomach turns. I almost throw up.

I start shaking.

There's a knock on the door, and I nearly jump out of my skin. "Hurry up. I have to pee."

It's a girl's voice.

I open the door and there's Chloe. Her beautiful Asian face looks so young this morning without any make-up on. I notice a tattoo on her bare arm, a T and some numbers printed across her bicep. I step out, and she brushes past me and closes the door.

There's a box of donuts on the living room table. Serena is munching one of them.

"You need to know the rules," Tommy says. He's standing next to the coffee table and motions for me to sit down on the couch. "There are only three." He holds up a finger. "One: no stealing money. I will give you everything you need. Two: you belong to me now, so never, ever try to get away. And three, do what I say. If you obey those three things, you'll be okay. Any questions?"

I shake my head.

"Good. Now eat. You have a big day ahead of you."

My heart is beating so hard I think it might burst. My hands won't stop shaking. I wrap my arms around myself in a kind of hug.

Tommy shakes a pill out of a bottle and hands it to me. "Here. This will relax you."

I take it but don't put it in my mouth.

"I'd take that if I was you." It's Chloe. She's out of the bathroom. She sits beside me on the couch, and I notice her eyes are bloodshot and hazy, like my mom's get when she is taking the pills.

Tommy leaves the room, and it's just me, Chloe and Serena.

"I need to get out of here. I don't belong here," I whisper. "There's been some mistake. I'm not a prostitute. I was kidnapped."

Serena laughs. It's a small, bird-like sound. "You think any of us *want* to be here?"

I look over at her. She's clearly high on something. These girls are drug users. I'm a high school senior headed for college. This is *not* where I belong!

"Take the pill," says Chloe gently. She pats my knee soothingly with her hand, her brown eyes pleading. "It's better that way. Tommy knows what's best for you. He will take care of you. You'll see."

"How old are you?" I ask.

"Fifteen. I've been here two years. This is your life now. So just accept that."

"No," I say. "I'll get out."

Serena shakes her head. I notice she never meets our eyes. "No, you won't."

Chloe takes my shaking hand and pushes the pill up towards my mouth. Her hand is cold and clammy. "Then at least until you do, take the pill," she says. "Tommy will come for you soon, and you'll have to work."

Work?

"He expects you to make $1200 a day," Serena says, lighting a cigarette. "Don't come home until you do."

I really look at Serena for the first time. She has shoulder-length red hair that lays in ringlets around her face. Round blue eyes. A pale face with some freckles across her nose. Today she's heavily made-up. Dark eyeliner. Dark blue eyeshadow. Red lips that are leaving a stain on her cigarette.

"I don't do this," I say.

But Chloe hands me a bottle of water. I look at her. *Fifteen years old*. She's so young. What was I doing when I was fifteen? Studying, of course. And that's the year Brittney and I designed the homecoming float. The class voted for our idea over the others. The year she got her new puppy.

Tommy comes in the room. "It's nearly noon," he says. "You girls ready?"

Chloe looks at me and nods. A flash of new fear twists in my stomach. I stand, ready to run, but Tommy's sharp gaze cuts towards me. I touch my sore eye and glance back at Chloe, who is still nodding encouragingly. I put the pill in my mouth and she hands me the bottle of water. I swallow.

"You should eat something with that," Tommy says, tossing me a donut. I don't catch it fast enough, and it falls on the dirty carpet. Chloe picks it up and gives it to me.

"He's right," she says. "Eat something."

I take a bite and force myself to chew and swallow. But they are wrong. They are all wrong. I'll get out of here, because I don't belong here. And because Brittany will get me out. We never let each other down. Ever.

Chapter 18

What I remember of the day is a nightmare. The pill lasted through half of it, and then it started wearing off. The pain and fear drove me to take another one.

Mom's "I don't care" pills.

Tommy brings us back to the house around 3 a.m. again. I smell of stale cologne and strangers. But all I've had to eat in two days is the burrito last night and a donut, so I eat a package of cheese and crackers, barely chewing through the haze of drugs.

When I crawl into bed some ten minutes later, I am sore and tired. Parts of me hurt that I barely knew existed before yesterday. I curl on my side and pull the thin blanket up over me. I'm cold. I'd like to shower, to wash the stink from me, but I can't find the energy.

I think about Cory. He set me up. How stupid I was to believe he really liked me. How stupid I was to drink that wine. Stupid, stupid, stupid.

I'm just a nerdy girl who could never get her nose out of a book. And I couldn't even get a 4.0 report card, no matter how hard I worked. A 3.8 GPA was the best I could do. How did I ever believe Harvard would want to admit me?

The word stupid keeps playing over in my head.

I hear a rustle, and someone sits on the edge of my bed. I freeze, my heart beating quickly in little rabbit beats. I'm so scared I start to cry all over again.

"It's just me," says Chloe's soft voice.

I peek out from under the covers. She's still wearing a dress, which looks more like a slip it's so thin and skimpy. She smells of cologne and cigarette smoke.

"I came to check on you, since today was your first full day," she says. She lays a hand gently on my back. "Did you take the pills?"

I nod, brushing the tears away with the back of my hand.

"It gets easier," Chloe says. "Tommy gives you the rough guys first. It's his way of breaking us in. Some of them like it a little rough, you know? Just let them have you. It's easier that way. But you'll get better clients soon. And repeats. I like the repeats because you know what to expect."

She rubs my back.

"And living here you get food. I was starving out on the street when Tommy found me. And I was so cold in the winter. Here we have our own bed."

She's talking like this is a place she wants to be. I raise myself up on my elbow so I can look at her. "But I don't belong here," I say. "I have a mom and a home. I was just about to graduate from high school and go to college."

"You were going to *graduate?*" Chloe says, her eyes wide. "Wow." But then she shakes her head. "Your mom and your friends…can you imagine if they found out you were here? And did you have a boyfriend? I mean, what would *he* think?"

"I didn't have a boyfriend," I say, then feel a stab of pain as I think of Cory.

"College would never let you in now. No boy would ever want you after what you've done. You're different now, Heather. There's no going back. What we do…people don't understand." Chloe's youthfulness disappears, and a serious knowing fills her eyes. "This is your life now."

I shake my head. "Never." I say.

Chloe gives me a little pat on the back. "Get some sleep," she says.

After she leaves, I lay back down. The drugs and exhaustion pull me into a dreamless sleep.

———

I awake the next morning to find Reg already up, smoking a joint on her bed. She's wearing a black, low-cut dress and has heavily lined her eyes in black liner. Her shadow is smoky purple, and her lips are painted a bright pink. She has teased up her close-cropped black hair. Reg is tall and thin, full of angles. Her high cheekbones are colored with blush. She's pretty and reminds me of the models I see in magazines.

"You woke up late," she says.

I sit and rub my head. I feel agitated and a bit like I have the flu. I wonder if it's from the pills I was taking.

"What *are* those pills?" I ask. The smoke from whatever she's smoking is thick in the air. I cough.

Reg shrugs. "Probably Oxy. This stuff is better." She offers me her joint again, which I refuse. "Or this." She hands me a juice-sized glass of water.

"What's this?" I say, swirling the water around.

"Coke."

At first, I think she means a soft drink, and I'm about to say, "No, it's not. It's clear," when I realize how stupid I'm being.

I hand it back to her.

She drinks it. Then she hands me a small paper packet. It's about the size of a quarter and taped shut. "Swirl it in some water and drink it." She grins. "The first one is free."

I lay it on my bed and go use the bathroom. There are two men in the living room. One is the thug I saw yesterday. And another guy I haven't seen before. Thug One and Thug Two. When I'm finished in the bathroom, I come back in the bedroom.

My hands are shaking more now, and I feel like I'm going to vomit. I lay back down on the bed and curl into a fetal position. "I think I'm sick."

"You should get dressed," Reg says. "Tommy will be mad if you're not ready to go by noon." She nods towards the dress rack.

Images of yesterday come back to me.

"I can't." I start to cry.

Reg picks the packet up off my bed and pours some of the powder into a glass of water. She stirs it with her finger until it dissolves. "Here. Drink."

"Hey girls, almost ready?" I hear Tommy's voice out in the hallway. Slivers of fear race through me.

I sit up and drink it without thinking. Reg takes the glass back and goes over to the rack. She pulls out a green dress. It has sequins on it and looks like something a hooker would wear. "Put this on."

I lean back against the headboard. "I can't. I'm sick."

"We don't get sick days," she says. "This isn't school."

"How long have you been here?" I ask, pulling my knees against my chest to try to calm the shaking.

Reg shrugs. "Doesn't matter. What matters is I'm ready to work. And you aren't." She hands me the dress again.

I'm starting to feel better. The nausea is receding, and I realize that my hands are no longer shaking. I hold them out in front of me to check. Nothing. Nice and steady.

"Hmmmm," I say.

Reg quirks an eyebrow as if to say "I told you so." Then hands me the dress, and I stand to put it on.

"So…what do we use for birth control?" I hear my voice, and it sounds so matter-of-fact. Like I do this every day.

"Birth control?" Reg laughs. "Oh, honey, you have a lot to learn."

"No. Seriously," I say.

Part of my brain realizes I'm high. The other part suddenly doesn't care.

Reg walks over to her dresser and pulls out a box of condoms. She hands me two.

"Most of the guys won't want to use them," she says. "But here. Knock yourself out."

I take them and stick them down into my bra. And just in time. Tommy comes to get us then.

— — —

During Freshman year, we had to take Health class, which was a thinly disguised title for Sex Ed. Poor Ms. Peterson got stuck with teaching it to a bunch of giggling fourteen-year olds. But in all fairness, we did study other "health topics" as well.

Healthy eating was one section we covered. The irony of this class was that Ms. Peterson brought in snacks every Friday. The first week it was brownies. On Halloween she bought some pumpkin-shaped sugar cookies with orange sugar coating. The Friday after that she brought in her children's Halloween candy. And candy canes for Christmas. You get the idea. All while learning about eating our veggies.

Then we studied exercise. After that was, of course, a section on anti-bullying and mental health issues. And drugs.

Then, just as spring and the mating season arrived, we talked about sex.

Ms. Peterson did her best to keep us attentive. She handed out Jolly Rancher candies to us at the end of each class if we paid attention and didn't giggle too much.

I'm not sure what they thought they'd accomplish. There was a whole section on why we shouldn't have sex. They talked about all the gross diseases we could catch, and statistically what percentage of us already had them. Fun. And pregnancy. Let's not forget about *that* risk.

Then, after telling us why we *shouldn't* have sex, they passed out condoms, and poor Ms. Peterson had to demonstrate how to put one on a banana.

Brit and I giggled through the whole class because we were silly freshman girls, and that's what we did at that age.

The one thing they don't teach you is how to fight off a guy if you *don't* want to have sex. Shouldn't self-defense be part of the class?

I think it should.

Chapter 19

Tommy takes Chloe with us today. We're both in the back seat, and his creepy friend Franco, Thug One, is sitting in the front. Franco is huge, twice the width of Tommy, and he doesn't seem very smart. He doesn't say much, grunts his answers, and wears sleeveless t-shirts to show his bulging, tattoo-covered biceps.

At the hotel, Tommy grabs my wrist and escorts me to the hotel room. Even though I'm high, I dig my heels into the pavement and refuse to move.

"I won't do this," I say.

Tommy pulls harder on my wrist until he's literally dragging me from the car to the hotel room door. He opens it and throws me inside. I land on the floor, skinning both of my knees and reopening yesterday's scab.

"Yes, you will," he says.

He shuts the door, and I try to think. The drugs, lack of food, and lack of sleep have all made my brain hazy. But I come up with a plan. I'll talk the next guy into letting me use his cell phone. Then I'll call for help.

I'm under the blanket, wearing my skimpy dress but still trying to cover myself, when the first man walks in. He stands above the bed, looking down at me. He takes his wallet out and is tossing some cash on the nightstand. In the car, Chloe told me it should be $100 each time. Am I supposed to count it to be sure it's all there? No one has told me.

"Can I borrow your phone?" I say. My words are slurred. I remember that I'm high.

"Who you going to call?" he asks.

Suddenly, "help" sounds like a stupid answer. I stutter, trying to come up with something convincing so he'll turn over the phone. And then what? Will I dial 911?

"I'll order us some beer," I lie.

"You paying?" he says.

I nod. But he laughs.

"I didn't come here for beer," he says. He smells like he's already had one, anyway. He takes his phone out of his pocket and sets it carefully out of reach. Then he sits on the bed and reaches towards me. I cringe and feel tears running down my cheeks. He doesn't seem to care.

Maybe he'll fall asleep afterwards, I think. Then I can grab his phone.

But he doesn't. Nor does the next man.

Tommy comes in briefly between the third and fourth man. He stands near the foot of my bed, hands on hips. Through the drugs, I vaguely realize I'm naked. I pull the covers up around me.

"If you don't quit crying, we're going to lose clients," he said. His black eyes are steely and cold. "And that would be bad. *Very* bad. Got it?"

I nod.

I'm hoping he'll leave, but Tommy stands there at the foot of my bed, watching me for a moment. Then he sits down on the foot of it. He's close to me. I can smell his musky aftershave and see a faint scar under his left eye.

"You really thought he loved you, didn't you?" Tommy says.

At first I'm not sure who he's talking about. But then he continues.

"Cory is like that. Savvy, charming. He uses people to get things done. I'm so sorry you met him. If you had met me first, things would be different."

They would, I think. *I wouldn't be here. I would never have been drawn in by a creep like Tommy.*

Tommy leans forward and touches my hair. I pull away.

"You shouldn't have been messing with a college boy. But then again, you *are* a high school senior. One would think you would know better by now, not get pulled into his schemes. You're naive. Been raised in a sheltered world."

"I'm not naive," I say. "Cory was a jerk." Anger rises up in me. I have never hated anyone more than I hate Cory at that moment. The way he played me. What a fool I was.

"But you're here with *me* now," Tommy says. "I take care of my girls."

"I don't need you to take care of me," I say, the anger for Cory spilling out onto Tommy.

But he doesn't seem affected by it. He remains calm.

"But you do," he says. He gives me a sympathetic look. "You aren't ready for the world. Look at you. Look how hard you tried and just couldn't get good grades. And your mom. Don't you think if she really loved you that she would get better? She was apparently just in this for your dad, and when he died, she checked out."

Cory must have told him that my dad died. My hate for Cory grows stronger.

"What about your friends? Nobody has come looking for you yet."

"That's because they don't know where I am!" I say, defiant. I hate Tommy. I hate him so much.

"Why not? Didn't you tell them you were going to New York? Or did you just run away?"

That stops me. I did tell them. Dennis and Aaron and Brit. They know where I was headed.

"And surely they've seen Cory's hot car," he says.

I told Brit the color and model. *A red Corvette,* I had bragged.

"So if they knew that, they had enough info. And yet, here you are," he says. "It's not uncommon. I mean, as seniors they're focusing on graduation and moving on. They can't help that you ran away from your troubles."

"I didn't run away," I say. Or did I? I didn't tell my mom where I was going. I had been blowing off my studying these past few weeks. Had I given up?

"No?" Tommy says. "Hmmmmm." He stands up and walks around to the side of the bed. Then he turns to look at me. "Heather, you need to face the facts. You're nothing

84

and yet I'm here for you. When nobody else is, when your boyfriend dumps you, when your family doesn't come looking for you, *I'm here*. I am your constant. I feed you. I have given you a place to live—"

"—it's a prison!" I shout. "There are bars on the window!"

"To *protect* you," Tommy says. He jerks his thumb towards the door. "If you go wandering around there alone, someone will grab you. And you will be in a world of hell that I am trying to protect you from."

"A world of hell?" I say. "You make me go with strangers."

"Who are good to you. Nobody has tried to kill you. All they want is a little love. You have something to give, and it brings in money so we can survive. It's what you *do*, Heather. It's all you're good for. And nobody is coming to look for you. *Nobody.* Cory probably fed them a few lines about you running away, and I'm sure they have given up on you. With his charming good looks, he can be quite convincing." His voice grows quieter, accusing. "But then you know that."

Tommy walks towards the door. He looks back at me.

"Those strangers you say I make you go with? At least I choose who sees you. Out there," he turns, and points to the door again. "Out there you're at the mercy of the streets. And believe me, this is child's play compared to what would happen to you out there."

I swallow. I have no more words. Fatigue and sadness are overwhelming me at the moment, reaching through the drugs to claw at my heart.

"I'm here for you," Tommy says. Then he turns back towards the door and leaves. I'm alone in the hotel room.

Is it true that nobody's looking for me? I can't believe it, and yet here I am. I've been here for days. I don't understand why they haven't been able to track Cory down yet and through him, track down Tommy.

Maybe my mom is so deep on drugs that she can't think straight. Or maybe she is so depressed she no longer cares. Without me, she has it easier. No one to condemn her. No one to take care of. To feed. To feel guilty about neglecting.

But I know my mom loves me. I *know* she does. Things just changed after Daddy died. She can't help it. She's just hurting.

And Brit. I can't imagine she would forget about me. We promised to always be there for each other. But I didn't listen to her when she told me not to go off with Cory.

I put my head in my hands. What have I done? Have I brought this on myself? I certainly made enough mistakes. I never should have dated in the first place. I should have worked harder to get good grades. And I never should have run away without telling Mom where I was going.

That's me. A loser. A run away. A stupid girl.

Maybe I do deserve what I've gotten. Maybe I do deserve to be here.

What if Tommy is right? What if this is all I'm good for?

And then the door opens. Another man comes in. This one is dressed in a business suit. He looks at me and grins. The fight is out of me, and I allow him to have me as I force my mind into a place that is far beyond the motel room. The drugs take me away, and I don't remember much after that.

I crawl into my own bed as soon as Tommy brings us home. I want to shower the filth off of me, but I can't. Instead, I curl into a ball and cry.

Chloe comes in to my room.

"Here," she says. "You have to eat. You'll feel better."

The warmed burrito smells good. I haven't eaten all day. Since last night, maybe? I'm getting the days and nights mixed up because we work until the early hours of the morning. Sometimes either Chloe or Serena begins their day as I'm coming in. There are men who want them on their way into work.

I sit up and take the burrito from Chloe.

"What day is it?" I've lost track of time, but I think I've been here about three days.

She shrugs.

I left from home on Friday, which seems like a lifetime ago. Then spent the night at Cory's. And two nights here. So it's Monday?

A wave of relief washes over me. Mom will realize I'm not home. She'll call Brit's mom. Someone will be looking for me! And Brit…she'll know the make and model of Cory's car. They will find me! Maybe even today!

"Why are you smiling?" Chloe asks.

I shake my head. "Nothing," I say. "Nothing." Because I don't want to tip them off. Maybe when they come, I'll take Chloe with me. She needs to get out of here too. It'll be good.

I eat the rest of my burrito and fall asleep as soon as Chloe leaves. I'm feeling better, knowing that by morning, my help will arrive, and I'll be able to go home.

I don't wake until nearly noon. Reg is shaking me. "Get up and shower. You stink."

And no one has come for me. But soon they will. I know it will be soon.

Chapter 20

The next morning I'm sitting in the living room. I got up on time, got dressed and ready, and even borrowed Rag's dark eyeliner for my eyes. I've learned that if I don't fight, I don't get hurt. And I'm just biding my time. I'm even eating a donut because I'm sure that any moment my help will arrive. They've realized by now that I'm gone and have gotten the police involved. They can track down Cory's car. And my phone signal which must have pinged at Cory's house last. Right? Or however that works.

I look at Chloe and Reg. They are thin and look tired. Reg, slumped back on the couch, is eating a donut and smoking a joint at the same time.

Serena is out. She had the early shift.

When Tommy drives me to the motel room, my heart sinks a little bit. I thought the police would be here by now.

"What are you looking for?" Tommy asks.

"Nothing," I say. I try to quit searching for a familiar car, or a police car. I don't want to tip him off that they're coming for me.

When I get in the hotel room, I feel a little more desperate.

"Let them have you. It's easier that way." I hear Chloe's voice in my head. And that's what I do while I wait for help to arrive.

Halfway through my shift, Tommy comes in. My pill is wearing off, and I am shaking. I'm so scared I can hardly breathe.

"Am I done?" I say. That can be why he's here. He has come to take me away from this. Back to the house. At least there, no one hurts me.

But he shakes his head. Then he goes to my purse and counts the money I've collected so far today.

"How you doing?"

I pull the covers up around me. I'm naked underneath. Tommy likes for us to get dressed in between clients, but I didn't have time.

I shrug and don't meet his eyes. I'm trying to be tough, but then the words come out.

"Can I be done today?" I say. I'm ashamed at how much my voice trembles. "Please?" I hear myself beg, and I hate it. Then I turn my head away, facing the wall, because I don't want him to see me cry.

"Have you made your quota?" Tommy asks.

He knows I haven't. But he stands there, waiting for me to answer.

I shake my head.

I hear him sigh, like I'm a child who doesn't want to do her homework.

Then he turns to leave. I hear the door shut and know that soon it will open again, and I will have to get back to work.

The blankets are worn thin, and I wonder if they are ever washed. There are stains on the mattress that look like blood. Back home, Mom used a fabric softener that smelled like citrus. I close my eyes and try to remember the fresh smell. It brings back memories of Daddy, and me waking up late on Saturday mornings, and pancakes.

Then I think about my cat Gracie and wonder if Mom is feeding her. Or if they are both dead now, starved because no one has checked on them. The sudden thought of my cat being dead upsets me so much I clutch the blankets hard, and my nails dig through them into my palms. The pain is a welcome relief, because it distracts me from my present situation.

It has been a few minutes since Tommy left. There's a spark of hope that my next client won't show up. And then I hear the door handle turn.

Chapter 21

Reg says sometimes, if you can get them high enough, they forget what they're there for. They pass out.

Reg says it's a chance for us to get some rest. But I think maybe it's a chance to grab their phone.

Three weeks later, I decide to try it, so I'm smoking a joint when the next guy comes in. Tommy gives us drugs regularly, to help us work. We're not supposed to save them, share them, or sell them. But I have to take the chance.

This guy is big, I mean *really* big. Like football player big. His eyes are dark brown, and he looks mean. He's dressed in khakis and a polo, so not a total slum, but he looks like he means business.

"Want some?" I say and hold up the joint. There's a haze of smoke around me, and I'm feeling unusually relaxed. I'm trying to look cool, reclining back against the headboard. I'm *not* cool— there's always fear inside of me, inside my stomach gnawing away at me. But it's muted by this stuff I'm smoking. Reg is right. This is pretty good stuff.

"I didn't pay for a drug addict," he says. "Is that all you are? You sell yourself so you can get high? Disgusting."

His nose crinkles like he smells something bad, and he grabs me by the ankle and pulls me until I'm lying flat.

Then he takes the joint out of my hand and throws it on the floor. He crushes it out with the heel of his shoe.

"Drug addicts disgust me," he says and slaps me hard across the face. The pain bites into my skin with a fierce burning. "You're a pathetic loser. That's what you are. I wouldn't screw you if you were the last woman on earth." He slaps me again, and my ears ring. *Never hit on the face.* I hear Tommy's words echo in my head. Never. It leaves marks. I've heard him tell at least a dozen men this. Tommy's gonna be mad.

The man pins my wrists down so I can't move, and he straddles me. But now he's not here to have sex. He's here to kill me.

I scream.

"Loser," he says, and one of his hands frees my wrist and wraps around my throat, cutting off my air. "Coke whore."

I take my free hand and try to beat him off, but my pounding has no effect.

He lifts his hand once again, and I gasp in gulps of air. I try to scream, but it comes out hoarse.

"Drugs will kill you. If you want to die, I'd be happy to help you out."

He pushes down on my throat again. Black spots swim in front of my eyes. This is it. This is where I die. Here, in this seedy motel room, wearing a slutty black slip and smelling like stale smoke and marijuana. There's almost a relief in this, that it's almost over. That I won't have to suffer any more. But my mom will never know what happened to me. And it can't end like this. It can't. The survival instinct kicks in, and I'm terrified now more than ever. I don't want to die. Not here. Not like this!

Just as I'm about to black out, someone hits him over the head from behind with a lamp. He roars and turns, jumping off of me. I sit up, gasping for air, holding my throat and breathing.

It's Tommy. Before the man can move, Tommy pulls a gun.

"*Never hit my girls*," he growls. He takes the safety off. "Now get out."

The man stands.

"Pay first," Tommy says.

"But I didn't—"

"*Pay*." Tommy's eyes are dark. His words are steel.

The man stands there for a moment, weighing his options, but Tommy's gun is pointed right at his chest. He gives in, tosses some money on the foot of the bed, and leaves.

Franco, Thug One, comes in as the man leaves.

"He's blacklisted," Tommy says to Franco, who nods and leaves. Tommy puts his gun back in his pants.

"You okay?" he says. He walks over to me and takes my chin in his right hand. He turns my face and looks at both cheeks, then lifts it and looks at my neck. Shaking his head, he goes into the bathroom. He comes back out with a cold, wet washcloth. "Hold this against your neck," he says. "It's starting to bruise."

I'm still coughing, but I do as he says. He has saved me. Tommy has saved me.

— — —

When Brittney and I were twelve, we packed some cookies and our dolls and took them down to the playground in our neighborhood. My mom had sewn us dolls when we were both five. She gave them the same skin, hair, and eye color as us, so they were like little minis. I named mine Amanda and slept with her every night. As I got older, she occupied a place on top of my bookshelf and still sits there today.

But the coolest thing was Mom also made us dresses to match the dresses the dolls wore. I wore mine to kindergarten the day I took Amanda in for show and tell, and I would have worn it every day if Mom would have let me. Brit and I wore those dresses threadbare, and I remember crying when I outgrew my dress.

At the age of twelve we were almost too old for dolls, but one day we decided to take them to the park with us and share a picnic. That turned out to be the last time we really played with them.

The sun was out and it was warm, a day in late August when summer had slowed down and the days of freedom from school were numbered. We picked some grass and piled it into a little house for our dolls. Then we got the apples out of the brown paper sack my mom had packed them in. I started slicing one with the paring knife she sent along. We were the only ones in the park, and the day was perfect.

Brittney was braiding a daisy chain necklace for her doll, and I was munching on an apple, when four teenage girls approached us. I didn't know them, but I vaguely recognized them as some high schoolers who rode the bus that went past my house.

"What do we have here?" one of the girls said in a sing-song voice. She wore skin-tight jeans and had too much make-up on. She looked like trouble.

She walked over and looked down at us. "Playing with dolls?"

She reached down and quickly grabbed Brittney's doll before we could stop her.

"This one is dirty," she said. She held it up for the other girls to see. They laughed. Then she looked down at me. "You're going to be dirty, too. It rubs off, you know."

We hadn't faced much racism in elementary school, but I knew it when I heard it. I stood up.

"Give me the doll back," I said.

The girl held Brittney's doll up by her hair. The hair that my mom had so carefully braided with purple ribbons. "Make me."

I grabbed for the doll, but she held it higher, out of my reach.

"Or maybe your friend here will make me," she said, and she used the "n" word.

I reached down and grabbed the paring knife.

"Heather, don't," Brittney said, standing up so she was beside me.

"Give me the doll back," I said again, this time through gritted teeth.

"Ohhhh!" said one of the other girls, pretending to be afraid. "This one's tough. What are you going to do? Stab us?"

"I'll make you bleed out," I said. I wasn't quite sure what that meant, but it sounded good. I heard it on TV.

"You ain't got the guts," said the first girl, taunting us. Her friends laughed.

I held up my left hand, and with my right hand sliced a gash in my palm. The blood spurted out, and I squeezed it so that it dripped impressively on the ground.

"Wanna bet?" I said.

The girl's eyes narrowed, and I could tell she was scared. "You're crazy," she said. "A real nut job." She turned to the others. "Let's go." She threw the doll at me, and it landed at my feet.

I stood my ground as they walked to the exit of the park, and I watched them disappear.

Brittney picked her doll up and dusted her off. Some of my blood had dropped onto the front of the doll's dress, where her heart was.

"Thank you," Brittney said.

"No problem." My hand was starting to throb.

Brittney spit on one of our napkins and tried to wash the blood off of her doll's dress. It only smeared.

"It's okay," she said. "Now she's kinda related to you since she's carrying your blood." Our eyes met.

Then she took the knife out of my hand and made a small cut on her own left palm. "Let's become blood sisters," she said.

We shook hands, our blood mingling. We did it because we were the best of friends, and because it was dangerous. We felt wicked cool.

Then we went home, and my mom took me to urgent care. I had to get seven stitches. That scar is still there today. A white crescent moon in the palm of my left hand, that reminds me who my best friend is.

Chapter 22

Tommy drives me back to the house. Chloe microwaves a frozen pizza pocket and hands it to me with a bottle of water. My throat hurts, so Tommy gives me some pills to help with the pain.

Then I crawl into bed and sleep like the dead. I never even hear Reg come in.

The next day I'm the first one up. I feel nauseated again, and very weak. I pull aside the curtain of the barred window, and I notice my hands are shaking. It's a rainy day.

I try to stand, but my legs almost give out. So I sit back down, and put my head in my hands.

What's wrong with me?

The anxiety is working its way back into my stomach. Fear grips me so hard all the time that it has become familiar. I almost don't notice it some days, but today it's terrible.

I look at the clock. It's 10:30 a.m. Tommy will come get us at noon.

I need something. I'm not sure what. But I need it.

"Reg," I whispered. She doesn't move. "Reg?"

She moans and puts the pillow over her head.

I stand again, this time more slowly, and make my way over to her bed. "Reg?"

Still, nothing. I wonder if she has any more of that powder on her. It made me feel so much better last time I took it.

I take a slow, deep breath to keep from throwing up. I'm about to ask her where it is when I decide to let her sleep. Maybe she has some in her nightstand drawer. I quietly open it.

There's a small plastic bag with some in it.

There's a water bottle on my own dresser that has a little bit of water left in it. I'm not sure how much to use, but I try to measure the powder out onto a small piece of paper, like I saw Reg do yesterday. I spill a little on the carpet because my hands are so shaky. Then I pour it into the bottle and shake it. I close my eyes and drink the mixture.

I'm not sure how much time passes, but soon the nausea starts getting better, and I notice my hands have quit trembling. I slide down on the ground to sit and think for a while.

— — —

I don't know when Mom started using drugs. Daddy died when I was ten, and the following year they put her on an anti-depressant. Life went on as normal for a while.

I turned eleven that June, and we had a small party at the house. Brit came, of course, and a few other friends from school. Mom baked me a cake. Then later that week, she started to feel tired. She started to sleep more. Sometimes she'd forget to wake me up for school, and she'd be late for work. Some evenings she went to bed right after dinner.

I thought she was sick. I told Mrs. Hudson about it, and she talked to her. Mom went to the doctor, and all of her bloodwork came back fine.

After that, Mom seemed to rebound. We had a good summer and a good start to the school year. But gradually, as the leaves started to fall, Mom seemed to be closing down with the season. As the days grew shorter and colder, she got quieter. She spent more time sleeping again. Over the winter she let go of her friends, one by one. Mrs. Hudson, Brit's mom, was the last to go.

"Why doesn't your mom return my calls anymore?" Mrs. Hudson asked me one day. It was the day before Valentine's day, and we were sprinkling red sugar on cookies. Mom used to do this with me, but this year she hadn't even decorated for the holiday. Nothing. It's almost as if she forgot to get on with life.

I shrugged. "I don't know. She's just really tired."

"I imagine it's hard being on your own," Mrs. Hudson said. "She must miss your dad so much."

I wanted to tell her that Mom *wasn't* on her own. She had *me*.

I had started cooking dinner when she was too tired, following the recipes on the back of the box, or inside the red and white checkered cookbook she and Daddy got for a wedding present.

Mrs. Hudson called more often, and Mom let the answering machine get it. One day she just showed up on our doorstep with a casserole.

"I had extra filling, so I made two," Mrs. Hudson said. It was March, and she was standing on our porch. The snow fell around her, landing on her shoulders. I stood by Mom as she took the casserole from Mrs. Hudson's hands.

"Thank you, Roberta. You shouldn't have," Mom said. She didn't even invite her in.

After that, Mrs. Hudson quit calling. Instead, she used a different strategy, asking me about Mom. Giving me pamphlets about a grief support group at her church. Sending notes home with me that had the phone numbers of therapists on them. I really wasn't sure how to answer her inquiries about my mother. All I knew was that Mom was tired. *All of the time.*

I gradually took over more of the housework, the cooking, and the shopping. Then, when I was fifteen, Mom started to rebound. She just got happier and started taking over the duties. She became Mom again, only not really. She was perkier, but her eyes had a strange, glassy stare to them.

So I shouldn't have been surprised when the Hudsons met me at my house one day after school. They told me my mom had been arrested for stealing drugs from the hospital.

The courts didn't send her to jail, but she had to go to outpatient rehab and Narcotics Anonymous meetings. For a while after that, I got my Mom back. The mom I had known for the first ten years of my life. The mom I had before Daddy died.

"I want to get better for *you*," she said. "*You* are my reason to live. I want you to have a good life." And for almost a year, things were awesome.

That was the first time. The second time she lost her job.

Now Mom is alone. She's back on drugs, not going to therapy, and I don't even know if anybody is bringing her groceries.

I wonder who she'll get better for now that I'm gone. What if she *doesn't* get better this time? Or what if she takes one too many pills by mistake?

My stomach tightens in a knot as I remember. Who will take care of her now that I'm gone? Will my mother die because I ran away for the weekend? Because I *lied* to her?

Tommy opens the door to our bedroom, and I realize that I'm still sitting on the floor in my t-shirt and undies. I blink, wondering where I've been. Reg is dressed and has her makeup on.

"You have five minutes to get ready to leave," Tommy says to me. With heavy legs, I slowly stand. The drugs have taken full effect now, and I feel pretty awesome. I see some of the powder on the rug and quickly brush it in to the carpeting with my foot. I'm not sure what Reg will do if she sees that I've used some.

"Let's go," Tommy yells from the living room. I shrug into a black dress and grab a pair of heels. And then I grab the little white baggie of pills that I keep under my pillow.

And I head out the door.

Chapter 23

Serena is gone again, with Tommy's man Sal (Thug Two), so it's just the three of us in the backseat. Chloe is in between me and Reg. As soon as Tommy starts the car, Reg glares over at me.

"*Thief*," she hisses. Her eyes are narrowed, and she's showing her teeth.

I know she means the cocaine. But because she looks so mad, I play dumb.

"What?" I say and shrug.

"You know *what*. I said the *first one* was free. The others you have to pay for." She holds out her hand, palm up.

"Reg," says Chloe in a soothing voice. "You know she ain't got no money. She doesn't deal."

"She'd better come up with some. Or else."

I swallow, feeling some fear, but the coke is numbing it. So I lean across Chloe and narrow my own eyes. "Or else *what?*" I say. I have no idea what I'm getting myself into, but I feel I need to take a stand.

Chloe puts a hand on my shoulder and gently pushes me back. "You don't want to find out," she whispers.

Reg is leaning across Chloe. She whispers to me. "Tonight you die."

But Chloe puts a hand on Reg and gently pushes her back. "Reg, honey, she don't know," Chloe says. "She won't do it again. Right, Heather?"

"What are you girls talking about back there?" Tommy yells from the front seat.

"Nothing, Tommy. Just work stuff," says Chloe. She lowers her voice. "She'll pay you back, but you have to give her time."

Reg's eyes are glaring at me and look pretty deadly. I feel the fear inside of me stirring again. It wouldn't be a stretch for me to believe she'd actually kill me. I didn't exactly consider her my friend, but I thought we were at least on the same side. Apparently only if I keep my hands off of her stuff.

Chloe is reaching down inside her small purse. She pulls out a joint. "Here, Reg. Take mine."

Reg grabs it. "This isn't blow," she says.

"It's better."

Reg and Chloe stare at each other for a moment. I realize then that my life is hanging in the balance. I forfeited it when I took Reg's drugs. Chloe is trying to buy it back.

After a beat of silence, Reg shrugs and stuffs the joint in her bra. "Fine. Whatever. This time I'll let it slide. *This* time."

Chloe turns to me and gives me a tight smile.

"But what are *you* going to do now that you gave me your stuff?" Reg says to her.

Chloe shrugs. "I'll manage."

I think of the baggie of pills I have in my own bra. Tommy refilled them for me. I should offer Chloe some of mine. Because that's how we get through the day.

I start to open my mouth to speak, but Chloe quickly pats me on the knee. "I'm good," she says.

And then we're quiet for the rest of the drive.

Despite the coke in my system, my throat is still sore and the bruise under my eye is tender. I also have a bruise around my neck, which Tommy isn't too happy about. He likes for us to look pretty. And I suspect if we look beaten, it will arouse suspicion. Not that I think any of the creeps who come to us for sex really care.

I look out the window at the people on the streets. It's rainy and cold, and most of them aren't clothed well. Only one that we pass has an umbrella.

There are mothers waiting at the bus stop, with little kids in tattered clothes and no coats. They look cold. On the street corner just before our hotel, I see two young women standing, selling themselves. On another corner is a man who is holding a tin can, hoping for a handout from people who have nothing to give.

It makes me think of Brit. She would open her purse and dig into the depths of it until she found a few loose coins or a stick of gum. Or now that she's older and has a job, some actual green cash.

Brittney liked causes.

The first cause she took on was when we were in third grade. My parents took me to the Humane Society to get a kitten. They invited Brittney to come along because we did pretty much everything together. Also, Brittney had always wanted a kitten too, but her parents didn't. This was probably as close as she would get to picking out her own.

There were so many kittens to choose from! I narrowed it down to a little gray kitty with white paws, and a tabby with a white chest. Both were female, and both were very cuddly. I couldn't decide, and my parents told me I could only have one.

"But they're sisters," Brittney said. I'm not sure if that was true or not, but the kittens were sharing a cage.

"We can't separate them," I said, now determined to have both kittens. I couldn't imagine the kitten leaving her sibling or her best friend.

But Mom still said no.

Dad, though, got that funny smile that he got when he had a plan. He stepped out into the hallway, and I saw him pull out his cell phone.

I was holding the little grey kitten, and Brittney was holding onto the tabby. Both were purring loudly and cuddling happily in our arms.

"Which one do you like best, Mom?" I asked. I could tell her resolve was weakening.

She reached out and scratched the tabby behind the ears. It rubbed its face against her hand. Then she reached over to the gray I was holding and scratched under its chin. It lifted its little head in pleasure and purred louder.

I could tell Mom was swaying in her opinion of only one kitten. Brittney and I exchanged hopeful glances.

"I wish I could have one, too" Brit said, cuddling the little tabby closer.

"You can come visit it," I said.

Dad stepped back in the room, then. He had a huge smile on his face.

"I just spoke to your parents, Brittney," he said. "They think you should probably take one of the kittens home with you so it's not missing its sister too much. They can visit that way."

"*What?*" Brittney's whole face lit up and we both squealed, startling our kittens.

"You mean she gets one, too?" I asked, hardly believing our luck.

Daddy nodded and Mom smiled. I could see the relief on her face.

We were *so* excited. We decided to take the kittens we each were already holding, so I got the gray one, and Brit took the tabby.

A volunteer took our kittens into the back to put them in a travel box, while we went up front to fill out adoption papers. There was a lot of paperwork, and Dad paid the fees. Then, after what seemed like forever, the volunteer carried our kittens out in separate boxes and handed them to each of us.

We stopped at the store up front to buy water bowls and litter boxes and some food for the kittens. We even picked out a toy mouse for each of them.

As we were getting ready to leave, Brittney saw a sign on their bulletin board. It was a photo of a kitten who'd had his back leg amputated. "HELP SAVE WALDO" it said. He needed further rehab, and they were asking for funds. There was a small box for donations.

"Mr. Thomas, look," Brittney said, pointing at the poster.

Daddy paused and read it. "That's so sad," he said. "But I can't donate anything today. I've already spent enough money, and I'm out of cash."

Our kittens were unhappy in their boxes, so Mom suggested we get them home.

Later that evening, after she got the kitten settled in her home, Brittney came over. She had a bag full of crayons, scissors and paperboard. "We're going to raise money for Waldo," she said.

"How?" I asked.

"We'll start with a lemonade stand," Brittney said.

So we worked to make signs that evening. My kitten, which I named Gracie, helped us by standing on the paper and batting at the crayons.

That weekend we set it up and made $10. My dad drove us to the Humane Society's store to put it in the donation box. Later that week, Brittney called and learned that Waldo had gotten everything he needed and would eventually go out to a foster home.

That was the beginning of Brittney's causes.

She started raising money every summer for the Humane Society, usually through lemonade stands and garage sales. In the winter she helped with the soup kitchen that her church had once a month.

In fifth grade, when they were going to cut down the 100-year-old oak tree near our park to build a swimming pool, Brittney started a campaign to save it. The township moved the pool over several yards to accommodate the tree.

In middle school, she started volunteering at a little kids' camp in our neighborhood, and in ninth and tenth grade she went back as a camp youth counselor.

She did what she could to help causes.

— — —

The streets that we drive down today are full of causes. There are so many people for Brittney to help, I wonder where she would start.

Maybe she would start with me.

Chapter 24

Daddy died when I was ten, just six months after I got Gracie. It was December eleventh. The snow had all melted, and he was going out for a run.

It was a Saturday morning, and I was watching *Scooby-Doo Mystery Incorporated* on television. I had a bowl of cereal on my lap, and Gracie was cuddled up next to me, hoping for a taste. Mom had started a load of laundry.

"I'm going for a run, Heather-bear," Daddy said. I nodded but didn't say anything because I was sucked into my show. They were about to solve the crime and reveal who the monster was.

I heard him leave, and Mom came from the basement, where our laundry room was. "Did Daddy go for a run?" she asked.

I nodded.

Mom grabbed a dust cloth and started in on the furniture in the living room, careful not to block my view of the television. Then she moved into the other rooms, and I heard her humming.

My show ended, and another episode started. I finished up my cereal and flipped the channels until I found another show to watch. About halfway through it, Gracie curled up on my lap, and I was cuddling her, watching television and thinking how good life was.

Near the end of that show, I heard the doorbell. Gracie knew the doorbell meant strangers, which she didn't like. She scurried under the couch.

I saw Mom hurrying back into the living room to answer the door.

104

"Heather, mute that for a minute," she said. She was a bit out of breath from cleaning.

Mom opened the heavy front door, and I saw a look of shock on her face. I got up and quietly walked over to stand beside her. She was staring out the front door but hadn't made an effort to open the storm door.

There were two policemen standing on our porch They had their hats off and were holding them in their hands.

"Ma'am," one of them said. His voice sounded muffled through the glass.

Mom swallowed and pushed the storm door open. "Can I help you?" Her voice had a tremble.

They asked to come in. She let them. Mom had grown very pale.

"Ma'am, we have some terrible news," one of the officers said.

And that's when they told us Daddy died.

He was running and apparently had a heart attack. A driver found him beside the road, near Forest and Park. The driver called an ambulance, but Daddy was already gone. They needed for Mom to come and identify the body.

That's the day my entire world changed. I thought it was the worst thing that could happen to me.

I am crying when Tommy comes to pick me up. It's only 2 a.m., but I've made my quota for the day. He's drunk. I can smell it on him and see it in the way he staggers to the car. He doesn't ask why I'm crying or what's wrong. I mean, what *isn't*?

He drives me back to the house, but the other girls aren't home yet. I drag myself into the shower and wash the nastiness off of me, then crawl into bed without even drying my hair. I'm still crying. Not big tears. Just little, silent tears.

After a while, Tommy comes into my bedroom and closes the door. He walks over to my bed and lays down with me, something he has never done before. He pulls the covers up over us both, up to our chins. He's only wearing a t-shirt and boxer shorts.

He frees his hands from the blanket and lights up a joint. I've learned to identify some of the drugs by smell, so I can tell that it's pot, but he always has something else mixed in with it.

105

I am lying, curled on my side, watching him through eyelids half-closed. I pretend I'm asleep so maybe he'll leave me alone. I'm not sure what he's doing here.

He's quiet for a few minutes, taking long, slow drags on the joint. Then he hands it to me. "Here," he says. He's high. His speech is a little slurred, and his eyes are half-mast.

It's never a good idea to refuse Tommy, so I reach for it and take a few drags.

Then he rolls over to face me and starts kissing me gently on the face. He takes the joint from me and sets it on my nightstand.

Then he makes love to me.

— — —

I don't know what I think about sex. It's not an act of love for me. It's a job, one I don't have a choice in, and it usually involves pain. But with Tommy, somehow, it's different.

"Do you love me?" he asks, as we lay there together, smoking the joint again.

I don't know what that means. Of course I don't love him. I hate him.

"Yes," I answer. Because that's what he wants to hear. And because my feelings about him are confusing.

"My old man called me today," he says. "It's my birthday, and I thought maybe for a minute, he remembered. But he wanted money. I haven't heard from him in six years, and he called *because he wanted money.*"

Tommy takes another drag on the joint, and I think he's finished talking. My head feels floaty. I look up at the curtains covering the bars on my window, and I am almost asleep when he says, "I thought I got rid of him years ago. But today he calls. Today, of all days, and doesn't even remember."

Tommy swears. He cusses his dad from here to tomorrow. His anger is starting to scare me when he turns over to look at me. His eyes are red. "He used to beat me senseless," he said. "Beat my mom senseless. She was so stupid for staying. Then he left us when I was fourteen. Do you know how hard it is to grow up without an old man?"

106

I do, but I don't say that out loud.

There's a tear on Tommy's cheek. He brushes it away. Then he lays his head on my chest.

"Do you know how hard it is to grow up without an old man?" he repeats. He lays there for a while, and I lay still, not wanting to break up the moment. I hear him sniff a little bit and rub his eyes with the back of his hand. Then, after a few minutes more, he falls asleep. I know this because I can hear his breathing change. He has passed out.

I must pass out, too, because later, when Reg comes in, I wake up, and Tommy is gone.

Chapter 25

"We need some new clients," Tommy says the next day. Instead of driving us to the motel, he takes three of us to a street corner. Serena stays behind to go somewhere else with one of Tommy's men.

I've learned that he has other girls. His "wifeys" is what the thugs call them. The girls stay in other houses, and he travels around pimping them out. I have no idea how many of us there are, but he must be making a lot of money off of us.

We don't see a penny of it.

The street corner he drives us to is in a run-down part of the inner city. I'm still not sure which city we are in, but I think it's somewhere in New York because most of the cars I do see have New York plates. And it's definitely somewhere that there are four seasons. It's warmer outside today, and I wonder what the date is. I've lost track of time, but I think I've been here about a month.

I'm wearing a red low-cut dress and heels. Reg and Chloe are both in black. Chloe has fish-net stockings on.

Tommy hands each of us a business card with the name of a hotel on the front of it. "Have them take you here," he says. "The room number is on the back."

After he leaves we compare cards. We all have different room numbers.

Chloe gets picked up first. A white man wearing a dark blue suit coat. Maybe in his forties. He has a wedding ring on.

"We should leave," I say. But Reg is busy lighting her joint. Instead of replying, she takes a long drag off of it. Then she hands it to me.

I inhale and give it back to her. "I mean, what's to stop us?"

Reg shrugs. "Where would you go?"

I look around. The buildings are all boarded up. There are some shady looking guys standing across the street in front of a closed party store. They are wearing colors that I've learned to associate with a gang. One sees me looking at him and whistles. I quickly look away.

She's right. Where would I go?

I'm starting to get cold. It's warmer outside, and the days are getting longer, but my dress is sleeveless, and my heels are open-toed.

Spring means the prom. I wonder if Brittney is going, and if she chose that dark blue dress she was eyeing at Bingham's department store.

Prom and high school seem like another world ago. Did I ever belong to that world?

— — —

I remember the last time I stood on a street corner.

It was last fall, and we were raising money for prom decorations by holding a car wash. Brit and I were part of the fund-raising committee. We started early in the year so we could have a really rad prom, and we hit our budget by January of this year. The car wash took place in the parking lot of our mall, and they let us stand on the corner holding up signs to advertise. There were a lot of cars coming in.

It was a warm day in September, and all of us girls wore our bathing suits. Principal Make-it-So said we couldn't wear bikinis, but some of the girls did, anyway. They wore tiny little shorts to cover the bottom part, so I guess it was good. Besides, the principal never showed up. He was probably at his own kid's soccer game or something.

So there we were, Brit and I and a few other girls standing on the street corner. Brit and I were in a one-piece, but we were still causing a stir. I mean, what young guys wouldn't want to get their car washed by a bunch of senior girls clad in their bathing suits? We got a lot of whistles when cars drove by, and we laughed and waved them in. I remember how fun it was at the time to be noticed by the guys. We felt sexy.

109

It was a fun day, and we got into water hose fights, and at the end Brad Simmons dumped a bucket full of soapy water over my head.

We raised $300 that day.

Now, I can make that in an hour.

——— —— ——

A car has stopped in front of us. The man is driving a sporty Lexus, and I wonder how he dares to bring it into this part of town. I guess he figures he can outrun anybody who tries to chase him down.

He rolls down his window. "Hey, sweetheart," he says. He's talking to me. "Why don't you get in?" He's wearing a polo shirt, and I see golf clubs in his backseat.

I reach for Reg's joint and take another long drag of it. Then I open his passenger door and climb in. I hand him the card with the hotel address on it, and as he pulls away, I can feel the drugs lifting me up into that world of I don't care.

Before I'm completely gone, I briefly wonder if Reg will be okay standing there by herself.

This guy falls asleep right afterwards. As I'm lying there, I start to wonder about my situation. For the first time ever, I'm unguarded. I don't think there's anybody waiting outside the door to kill me if I leave. Or waiting inside to beat me. I turn over so I'm facing the man next to me. He's snoring slightly, sound asleep. I feel a slight thrill in my stomach at what I might do.

His pants are laying on the floor next to the bed. I wonder if his phone is in there. All I need to do is make one call. Just one phone call. I know Brit's number by heart.

My heart starts pounding at the thought. I get up as slowly as I can and make my way around to his side of the bed. He's still breathing evenly. I quietly pick up his pants and stuff my hand down into the front pocket. Nothing but some tissue and his wallet. I try the next pocket, and there's his phone. He has it password protected.

But you don't need a password to call 911.

Suddenly Tommy's voice is in my head. "Don't let the police catch you. You're a drug addict now. You'll get years in prison and a hefty fine, and that doesn't even include your prostituting charges."

But years in prison might be better than this.

They'll beat you in prison. Nobody wants you now, Heather. You're lower than dirt.

I push the voice aside and press the button that says "EMERGENCY" It opens to the keyboard screen so I can call. My hands are shaking.

"Hey!"

I jump so quickly I drop the phone. The man is sitting up, looking at me. "Are you trying to steal my phone?"

I shake my head. "No," I say. "No. I want to call for help."

"Help?"

He doesn't seem to understand. I find my dress and shrug myself into it. I'm really scared now. My heart is pounding in my chest so hard, I think it might burst.

"What do you mean, help?" he says.

"I don't want to be here," I say. It's now or never. I've gone this far, and there's no going back. Our eyes meet. He looks confused, but then he says something to me that I've never heard from another of the Johns.

"Are you being held here against your will?" he asks.

I nod and grab the money off of the dresser. I hear him saying "wait!" but I don't because now I'm terrified. He's just like all the others. He will only hurt me.

I open the door and run out, not taking the time to look for men lingering near to grab me. I just run. The rough blacktop of the parking lot cuts into my bare feet, but I don't feel the pain. I turn down an alley and keep running. My heart is pounding, my lungs start burning from the effort, and I've only gone a short distance. I'm really out of shape.

The alleyway ends on a street, and I look both ways. Most of the shops are boarded up, but there's a bar to my left and a party store to my right. I choose the bar and make a run for it. There has to be somebody in there who will help me, or a phone I can use.

I remember people in movies calling cabs from bar phones. Do they even have phone booths anymore?

And I don't have coins. But I'm still clutching the $100 bill.

Suddenly a car stops, and a man jumps out of the passenger side. He's wearing jeans and a green t-shirt. He has a beard forming on his unshaven face and dark, glinty eyes. I recognize him immediately as one of Tommy's thugs. It's not Thug One or Thug Two. I don't know his name, but I know he's scary.

I turn back and zigzag across the street. The bar isn't far now, only about a half of a gym length from me, but I hear his feet pounding behind me. Fear races through me like a lightning bolt.

I put everything I have into going faster. The door to the bar opens, and a man walks out.

"Help me!" I scream, just as I'm jumped from behind. The force takes me down, flat on my stomach, and my chin hits the pavement of the street with such force that I think my neck will snap. Instead, I feel my teeth slam together.

He grabs me by the back of my hair and rolls off of me, yanking me up into a sitting position.

"Stupid!" he says. "Now Tommy's going to *kill* you!"

He slaps me hard across the face. The sting brings tears to my eyes. I reach towards the man who has walked out of the bar, but he looks away.

"Help me," I say, my voice weak. My lungs are fighting for breath. I feel like I'm about to pass out.

The thug drags me by my hair to my feet, and then he grabs my wrist. In a last effort for freedom, I kick him hard. I'm aiming for his balls, but I hit his knee instead. He howls in pain and throws me to the ground, kicking me hard in the side. The pain is unbearable, and I curl into a fetal position, clutching my ribs.

But he grabs my wrists again and yanks me back to my feet. He drags me towards the car, which the driver is moving towards us. Then he throws me in the back seat and climbs in next to me.

I don't know the man who is driving.

The thug next to me gets an evil grin on his face. "I wouldn't want to be you," he says. "Not when Tommy hears what you did."

I realize I'm still clutching the $100 bill. He reaches over and snatches it out of my hands and puts it in his pants pocket. Then he shakes his head. "Tommy ain't gonna be happy you didn't get paid for this lay," he says.

"But—"

As I start to speak, he slaps me again. I want to spit in his face, but I'm so scared that I cower down into the seat instead, as far away from him as I can get. I wish I was braver. I wish I was more.

Chapter 26

We soon arrive back at the house. The driver stops in front of the house so the thug can drag me out of the car. He pulls me into the house.

"Tommy!" he shouts.

"What's up, Nash, my boy?" Tommy comes through from the kitchen to the front room.

The thug, who is apparently named Nash, throws me on the floor at Tommy's feet.

"This one was running away," he said. "I caught her racing down the street screaming for help."

I'm lying on my side, clutching my ribs. Tommy looks down at me, and I see the anger in his eyes. "Is this true?" His voice is very quiet.

I don't say anything.

"And she didn't get paid. That last John got a freebie," says Nash.

"That's not true," I begin, but suddenly Tommy's boot kicks me right in my sore rib. I scream in pain.

"Don't speak!" Tommy says. He grabs my arm and hoists me up to my feet. "That will be all, Nash," Tommy says, without taking his eyes off of me. "You're free to leave. I'll see that you're paid."

I hear the door open and close. Tommy pushes me up against the wall and presses his body against me. His face is in mine. "You have no rights," he says between clenched teeth. His breath stinks of garlic, and I gag. "Do you understand? What did I tell you when you moved in here? That there are only *three rules*. You have broken two of them. Tell me what the rules are."

114

He takes both of my wrists and pins them up above my head, pressing me closer to the wall. My shoulder blades are digging into the drywall. His body is pressing into mine, his legs pinning mine against the wall.

"Tell me!" he shouts. I cringe and shut my eyes.

"The first one is no stealing money." My voice is shaking. I don't mention that I took the $100 or that Nash took it from me. I try to remember the other two and they come to me: "I belong to you, so never, ever try to get away," I say. I swallow hard. "And do what you say."

"You *do* belong to me," Tommy says. "No one else would want you. I take care of you, Heather. I *feed* you. *I buy you clothes.* I give you a home and a bedroom. And this is how you repay me?"

I turn my head to the side, to escape his breath and his eyes.

"I'm sorry," I say.

"I'm sorry, too," he says. "But now I have to punish you. You brought this on yourself."

He pulls me away from the wall and throws me across the room. The back of my legs hit the coffee table and I fall backwards across it. A sharp pain cuts into my back as I land on it, then tumble to the floor. Tommy is on top of me then, and he slaps me across the face, first on the right side, then on the left. I'm seeing stars, but he jerks me up to my feet and punches me in the jaw.

The blackness sweeps over me, but he grabs my hair and jerks me upright again. The pain in my scalp pulls me back to consciousness. No hitting in the face, I want to scream. It'll show. Then he throws me back on the floor and kicks me in the stomach, the ribs, the kidney.

The kidney kick hurts like nothing I've ever known. I remember from one of my science classes that kidney punches often result in peeing blood for a while. I wonder if that's going to happen to me.

Tommy grabs my wrists and drags me over to a door I've never seen open before. He unlocks it and throws me inside. Before I can catch myself, I'm falling down a flight of stairs. I land at the bottom, protecting my head with my arms, and end up splayed out on cold cement. He shuts the door and leaves me in total darkness.

I lay there for a long time, very still, waiting for my heart rate to slow. I try to go over what just happened, but it was all so fast. I stole. I brought this onto myself. If I had just stayed with that last John.

My breath is coming in ragged gasps, and that scares me. I pretend I'm a medical student, in the ER, and that this girl (me) has just came in. I need to assess her injuries.

My kidney hurts. Probably bruised. My ribs, probably cracked. It hurts when I try to take a breath in. But not completely broken because I can move my right arm upwards and my ribs feel like they stay intact.

After a few minutes, I slowly sit up. I feel a bit dizzy, but that passes after about a minute. I do have a bad headache now, from the hitting. I do a concussion assessment, based on what I learned during my freshman year when I played volleyball. I can't do the usual memory test because I have no idea what day it is, or what time it is, and my mind is still a little fuzzy from the drugs I took. I do know the current president, and I remember the name of my high school and my own name.

But I could be mildly concussed. I have a bad headache, but there's no way to tell if I have any double vision, because I'm in the dark. I can't see a thing.

What if I'm blind?

New panic starts my heart racing again. I wave my hand in front of my eyes, but still nothing. Then I squint upwards towards where I think the stairs are, and after a moment I see a faint glow under the door.

I'm not blind. I'm just in the dark.

I'm in a basement.

It's cold. I feel my way around to see if there's a chair, or a blanket, but after a few swipes with my hands they encounter cobwebs, and I pull back. I try to wipe the sticky stuff off of my hands, but it's hard to do, even on the sequined dress. I wonder if there are spiders. I hear myself whimper, and I pull my knees up against my chest and wrap my arms around them, making myself as small as I can.

116

I wonder what will happen next.

It's quiet upstairs, and I suppose the other girls are still working. I don't even hear footsteps, and I wonder if Tommy has gone. Maybe I could try going upstairs?

But no. the beating Tommy gave me...I don't want to risk that again.

I'll just stay here in the dark. Maybe he'll forget about me.

I try to think of happy thoughts. For some reason the first thing that comes to mind is last fall's homecoming. I didn't go because I had to work, and also because I had my no dating rule. Which I should have stuck to. Look what happened with Cory.

I'm so stupid.

— — —

Dennis wanted to ask Emily Watson to homecoming. Emily was way out of his league. She was a cheerleader, for starts. But she was probably the only sweet cheerleader, so I guess if he had to go for that type, she was the best to pick from. Emily was petite and blond and had big blue eyes. She didn't have a steady boyfriend, but she was always being asked to dances and usually showed up on somebody's arm. As far as I knew, she wasn't the kind of girl to sleep around. She was just nice, and pretty, and very popular.

But she wasn't the kind of popular that made her unapproachable. Unless you were Dennis.

Three weeks before homecoming he caught up to me by my car in the morning when I arrived at school.

"I want to ask Emily to the dance," he said. I just stared at him for a moment because it threw me completely off guard. I had no idea he had a thing for her.

"*Emily?*" I said, then coughed because I wanted to cover up the surprise in my voice.

"Yes," Dennis said. He started wringing his hands, a bad habit he had when he got nervous. "And I need your help."

"Me? Why me?"

"You're experienced."

"At *dating?*"

Because I certainly was not.

"No. I mean…experienced at being a *girl*."

I laughed. "I guess you're right about that. But why do you need me? Just go ask her."

Dennis gave me a withering look, like I was a dork. It was obvious. He was the school nerd and was ostracized by the football team. The only reason he hadn't been smashed by now was because of Aaron's friendship. I sighed.

"Okay. Come to my house after school. We'll figure something out."

I spent the day wondering what I would want from a guy if I was going to be asked to the homecoming dance. What would get *my* attention? I'd definitely want something romantic. I thought of all of the romance books I read and all the chick flick movies that Brit and I watched over the years. And finally, at the end of fifth hour, an idea came.

Dennis showed up at my house at 4:40 p.m. Mom wasn't home from work yet. She was in a good period, so there were ice cream sandwiches in the freezer. I got one for each of us.

"It has to be personal and something that is very *you*," I said. "And also very her. I'll stalk her a little bit and find out what she likes."

"Something very *me*…" said Dennis, thinking. He peeled back the paper on his ice cream sandwich and took a bite. His dark hair was tousled and wavy. He glanced over at me with his dark brown eyes and smiled. "You're such a good friend to help me out. Do you think I even have a chance?"

Dennis, as I said before, is kind of cute. He just needs to get his head out of a computer long enough to live a little.

"Of course," I said, taking a bite of my own ice cream sandwich. "I mean…at least a little bit. What does it hurt to ask?"

"Rejection is painful," said Dennis.

"Yeah, but aren't you rejected already anyway?"

"True enough."

We both nodded at his sad truth and took another bite of our ice cream sandwiches.

"So since you're like some kind of super dude with computer hacking, what if you created some kind of computer code that would run the question across her screen when she logged on?"

"The question?"

I put my hand against my forehead. *"The question!* You know, "'Will you go to homecoming with me?'"

"Oh." Dennis was quiet while he finished his ice cream sandwich. "I could do that," he said finally. "I know exactly how. She's in computer science with me, and I can hack into the entire system, and it will show up on everybody's computer...."

"Wait," I said. "That might get you expelled. What if you just hack into *her* computer?"

He was quiet for a moment. I could see the wheels turning.

"I can send her an email that will act like a virus. When she clicks on it, the words can pop up and scroll across her screen!"

"That's perfect!"

Dennis's enthusiasm was short lived. "But she'd never say yes. That's just another nerdy thing I'd do. She needs to get into me, you know. Notice me. Like me."

"That's the part I'm going to work on. I'll figure out what she likes, and you can send her little surprises for several days before the big proposal."

"Surprises?"

"Let me work on it."

So I spent the rest of that week discreetly stalking Emily. I sat next to her in class, followed an unnoticeable distance behind her in the halls, and listened in to her conversations with her friends. I even did some cyberstalking, looking at her Facebook and Instagram feed and even following her on Snapchat.

Dennis, meanwhile, got to work on his virus. We met again at the end of the week. He showed up at the coffee shop where I was working. I was ready with an arsenal of stuff.

"Her favorite color is pink," I said. "On Monday, leave a pink rose on the hood of her car with a note that says "'From your secret admirer.'"

"That's creepy."

"No, because you're going to add 'I want to ask you to homecoming. Will you think about it?' That way if somebody else asks her, she will know she might have something better waiting for her."

"Oh."

"She collects teddy bears," I said, pulling out an old Beanie baby of mine that still looked brand new. It had a note tied around the neck that said "To Emily."

Dennis opened it and read it. "From your secret admirer. Only two more days until I ask you to homecoming."

"You're building anticipation," I said. "You can leave it in a pretty bag hanging from her locker. With this."

I reached into my pocket for the rubber suction cup with a hook on it. I took it off the small stained-glass cat I have hanging on our kitchen window.

"Perfect." He grinned. I could tell he was impressed.

Then I pulled out a heart-shaped cherry lollipop. I had tied a note to it with red ribbon and curled the ribbon with scissors. The note read "You are sweet. Tomorrow I will ask you to homecoming. I hope you say yes! From your secret admirer."

I had typed the notes on my computer and printed them off so no one would know my handwriting.

"She always brings her lunch on Thursdays," I said. "I heard her talking to her friends about how she hates the Thursday cafeteria choices. On Thursday morning I'll ask her friend Anne to sneak it into her lunch bag."

"How are you going to do that without being seen?"

I shrugged. "I'll get a pass to the bathroom. Anne has a free hour then and will be in the library. She'll go along with it because she loves secrets. I remember that from fifth grade camp."

"But you're my friend. She'll guess."

"No, because I'm also Aaron's friend. It could be a guy on the basketball team who is interested."

Dennis nodded. "You're brilliant."

Mr. Sneeder had been sitting there, sipping his coffee and listening. "Sounds like quite a plan," he said. "That's sort of how I proposed to my wife. Only I bought her a train ticket and took her to Chicago for the Christmas window displays. I gave her some clues, and she had to guess her way through

120

the stores until she came to the jewelry counter where I had pre-purchased her ring."

"Awwwww!" I said. "That's so romantic."

Dennis rolled his eyes. "Heather likes romance."

Mr. Sneeder rolled his eyes too. "I know. She's always telling me about the latest romance novel she's reading. It's what the women like, my man. You've gotta know how to woo the women."

"I guess."

But Dennis's eyes were sparkling. He was excited, I could tell. I was pretty proud of my ideas myself. It was fun to plan out someone else's romantic adventure.

So on Monday, Dennis left the pink rose on Emily's car. There was a flutter in the cheerleader world as they talked and wondered who it could possibly be. Names were tossed about, the captain of the football team, the co-captain of the basketball team (Not Aaron – the other guy), or that really cute lacrosse player, the new kid.

On Wednesday, when she found the teddy bear in her locker right before lunch, she smiled so big I thought her face would burst. Dennis and I were watching from our own lockers nearby. "Scored!" I said quietly to him.

Then on Thursday, we sat at our lunch table and waited for Emily to open her lunch bag.

"She's gonna be creeped out," Brit said. "I mean, I wouldn't wanna eat any lunch that someone had pawed through."

Dennis looked worried, but I put my hand on his arm. "Brit's just jealous that Aaron hasn't thought of these things."

Brit smiled sweetly at Aaron, who was taking mental notes, I could tell.

We all watched as Emily pulled out her sandwich. She didn't notice the lollipop right away, and it was an agonizing ten minutes before she pulled out her chips and found it. She showed her friends and their heads turned, trying to figure out who this secret admirer was. Our plan was working out perfectly.

Then Friday came. Dennis had his virus ready. It was set to pop up both on the laptop she carried with her and on her phone, just to be safe. Dennis timed it for fifth hour so if she said "no," he could hurry home and hide. It was perfect because we had English lit that hour and would be using our laptops to write. Or those who had laptops. I had to use one of the school's Chromebooks.

Dennis and I sat together in agonizing silence while our teacher told us the symbolism behind Paradise Lost. Then we opened our laptops to write a short essay on said symbolism. My heart was beating quickly. I was scared for Dennis. And hopeful.

Dennis looked at me and swallowed. He was nervous. He was wearing a pin-striped button down, open a little at the chest, and khakis instead of his usual baggy jeans. I had told him what to wear today. I thought he looked pretty darn good.

He opened his phone and sent the email. It popped up on Emily's computer and phone at the same time. She glanced at it, then looked over at Dennis. "Open it," he mouthed silently.

She did. I was sitting two rows behind her and a bit diagonal from her, and I could see her screen light up as a large rose appeared on the dashboard. It slowly opened, and words spilled out from it. *"Emily. Will you go to homecoming with me? From Dennis – your secret admirer."* Then it had a brief slide show of the rose, the teddy bear, and the lollipop, after which the whole thing started over.

Katie, who sat behind her, could see the screen also, and so could a few other kids. As people noticed, I heard some small talk starting.

"Dennis?" someone said. *"That* nerd?"

Emily turned an interesting shade of pale, and then red. She swallowed a few times. I could tell she was trying to decide. He had won her heart, but her popularity was at stake.

Finally, she turned to him, smiled, and nodded.

I looked over at Dennis, who had a huge grin on his face. I sent him a quick text. "**Play it cool, dude,**" after which he tried to suppress his smile a little bit. Emily closed the email. Her face was still very red, but she was smiling.

So Dennis's parents sprang for a new suit, and he took Emily to the homecoming dance. They looked awesome together. Brit gave him a few dancing lessons, and he made it through the evening without messing anything up. Afterwards,

Dennis told us that Emily thanked him for a wonderful time and gave him a light kiss on the lips.

Nothing came of it. She talked to him now when she passed him in the halls, but they didn't become a couple. He didn't ask her out on any more dates, not wanting to press his luck, but he did ask her to dance with him at Snowcoming. And she said yes to one dance, even though she showed up with one of the basketball players.

Dennis was happy. And it felt super good to have been a part of that.

Chapter 27

Sometime during the night I fall asleep, but I wake up trembling from the cold. My arm is numb where my head has been laying on it. I sit up in the dark and search for the light under the stairs. I don't see anything. It must be totally dark upstairs.

I have that gnawing feeling of unease again, and some nausea. Probably from the concussion?

I wrap my arms around me, trying to stop the trembling. My heart is racing. A sudden wave of panic takes me. Clawy things are crawling across my skin. I brush at my arms.

I need help. I need to get out of here.

There are no widows. What type of basement doesn't have windows? I think about moving away from the stairs and looking for a door to the outside, like a cellar might have. But it's so dark. And I remember the spider webs.

I scramble around on my knees, looking for the stairs, feeling my way across the cold concrete floor. My entire body is aching, especially my head and my side. I find the bottom step and pull myself towards it. Then I make my way up the stairs, crawling. One step at a time.

The shaking is getting worse. I feel like I might throw up. By the time I'm at the top of the stairs, my whole body is racked with tremors.

"Tommy!" I try to choke out the words. My throat is dry and hoarse. I need help.

"Tommy!" I sit there, calling his name. I'll beg him to forgive me. I just need help. I *need* something. *Something.* I don't know what.

After what seems like forever, someone opens the door. I can't see because it's dark.

"Shhhh!" says a voice, and I realize it's Chloe. "You're having withdrawal symptoms. Here." She hands me a few pills.

"I need help," I say, pushing her hand and the pills away.

"Shhhh. If Tommy catches me here, he'll be mad. Take these. This is what you need." She folds them into my hand. "Take them, Heather, please."

The pleading in her voice, the tremors in my body, make me do as she asks. She hands me a glass of water to wash them down. Then she sits beside me on the step and holds my hand, waiting with me until my body quiets down. It couldn't possibly be withdrawal. I'm not a drug addict. I'm just cold and scared.

Eventually, the tremors stop, the shaking stops, and I feel the anxiety retreating.

"I'll see you soon," Chloe says, and closes the door. She locks it again, and I hear her footsteps move away.

I am once again alone.

— — —

I'm still sitting on the top step when Tommy opens the door. The bright daylight streams in, hurting my eyes. "Time to work," he says. He walks off, leaving the door open.

I get up shakily and walk to the bathroom, closing the door behind me. I hardly recognize the woman I see in the mirror. My left eye is circled in black, my bottom lip swollen. I still have the bruises around my neck. I take my dress off and look at my side. It's black and blue. I touch it and it's very tender. There are other bruises on my torso where I was kicked and beaten.

I run cold water and splash my face. There's a sharp knock on the door.

"Time to go!" Reg says.

"Hurry up, Heather!" I hear Tommy shout from the living room. "I don't have all day! Do I need to teach you another lesson?"

I wrap a towel around me and open the door. "I need to get dressed," I say. I hear Reg gasp as she sees my bruises, but I keep moving.

I find the least wrinkled and smelly dress in the pile on the bedroom floor and pull it over my head. Then I head out towards my day.

— — —

"What happened?" Chloe is working with me today. We're back on the street corner.

I shrug. I don't want to talk about it. It made me realize that there might be no escape from this world that I'm in. What did I do to deserve this? Where did I go wrong? I have lain awake many nights tracing my path. What I could have done differently. What I *should* have done differently.

I realize, finally, this morning at this moment, that I have been trafficked. I remember a television show, one of those crime shows where the good guys solve a crime and let the audience follow them along. It was about this missing girl, and the investigators followed all the leads. Eventually, they found her down near the Mexico border at some little town in Texas. She had been walking along the street one night looking for her drug dealer, and somebody picked her up. They sold her to someone else, and soon her life became a nightmare of being sold for sex. That's what's happening to me.

Only I wasn't looking for my drug dealer. I was looking for a way to get into college.

And now here I am. Sold. I don't even know which city I'm in. This city doesn't have any distinguishable landmarks. No big bridges or skyscrapers. Just endless rows of falling apart houses and buildings.

"Come on," Chloe says. "Tell me what happened. Did Tommy chop you?"

Chop. That's the word the girls use for beat. I've heard it before in conversation.

There's a wind today. I wish I had a coat to pull around me. Or a shawl. Anything. There are goose bumps on my arms. A car crawls by and two men wolf-whistle at us from inside, then they drive on.

"He only does that if you don't follow the rules," she says. "Don't make Tommy mad, Heather. Please."

I look over at her, finally meeting her eyes. She's so young. *I'm* so young. Aren't these supposed to be the best years of our lives?

"How do they find us?" I ask.

"Who?"

I nod as another car drives by.

"The men? Tommy runs ads. You know, in those online sites, like FindForSale.com."

"My mom sold a couch on there once," I say.

This time it's Chloe who shrugs. "I guess you can buy anything nowadays."

I see two men meet across the street. One pulls a baggie out of his pocket and hands it to the other, who gives him a wad of cash. Right in broad daylight. Where are the cops?

I never see cops.

"So why are we here on the street?" I ask. "If he runs ads?"

"Sometimes he likes to find fresh clients," Chloe says. "If business is slow."

As if on cue, a car stops. It's a businessman. He's wearing a suit and has kind eyes. And he's clean. Maybe he's less scary than some of the men I've been with already. Maybe.

I glance across the street where one of Tommy's thugs is leaning against the wall of the boarded-up pharmacy. Watching.

"I'll take this one," I say, because the next guy could be worse. And there's always a next guy. But then I have a flash of guilt over leaving Chloe for that "next guy."

I look over at her, and suddenly I'm afraid for her.

"Or do you want him?"

"No, you go," she says. She pulls a joint out of her bag and lights it. "I've got this to keep me busy."

I walk up to his car.

"Hop in," he says.

I tell him the hotel and room number. Along the way I see a sign with a smiling woman wearing a black graduation hat. "Turn Your Life Around at Community College," it says. Mrs. Peterson wanted me to go to community college.

When we get to the hotel, I see two of Tommy's men in the parking lot. So I open the car door and get out with this man.

I'm starving. I can't remember the last time I ate. As we walk into the room together, things spin, and for a moment I think I'm going to faint. I fall onto the bed, and he thinks I'm there for him.

He doesn't ask about my bruises. "Aren't you a pretty thing?" he says, grinning and taking his suit coat off.

I close my eyes and pray that it's over quickly.

— — —

I first wanted to be a doctor when I was three. Mom bought me a preschool-sized doctor's kit, which was under the tree for me when I woke up on Christmas morning. I was so excited! It had a stethoscope and a white lab coat. She had my name embroidered on the front pocket. There was a black doctor's case, like you see in the old movies, and when I opened it there were fake syringes for shots and a stethoscope. There were also bandages, which I found out later my mom had added in.

I loved it and played with it all of the time. My stuffed animals all had turns being "sick" and coming to the doctor so I could fix them up. Daddy was thrilled.

"You're just like your great-grandma Heather," he said proudly. His eyes always twinkled when he talked about her.

When I got a little bit older, my parents bought me the Barbie doll doctor and all the cool stuff that comes with it. Brit and I played with those sets for hours.

Daddy called me Dr. Heather Thomas on a regular basis.

"Dr. Heather Thomas, you are being paged. You're going to be late for school if you don't hurry," he would say on Monday mornings, when he drove me to school on his way to work.

"Dr. Heather Thomas, dinner is getting cold," he'd yell up the stairs when I was too busy playing to come when they called the first time.

I loved it. I loved that my parents supported my passion for medicine. I loved the time and energy they spent making me feel special—like I could conquer the world. We were so happy then.

Before Daddy died.

Chapter 28

None of the men ask about my bruises. Or my black eye. One did trace his finger gently around it and say "Fell down the stairs, huh? That happens to my wife a lot."

When I return to the house, Tommy grabs my chin. I flinch away from his grasp, but he holds it tight and looks closely at my eye. He just shakes his head.

Then he walks away.

I haven't eaten since sometime yesterday. I can't even remember.

Reg is in the kitchen smoking. She hands me her joint and without thinking, I take a hit of it. I'm so shaky I can't stand, so I sit down in one of the chairs. Reg riffles through the pantry and pulls out a few granola bars. She tosses me one. I try to catch it but it lands on the floor. I bend over to get it and drop her joint, which lands on top of my bare foot and burns a spot before I can grab it.

I sit up and hand it back to her, ignoring the new injury. Then I tear away the wrapper of the granola bar, devouring it as quickly as I can.

"How's your pain?" Reg asks in a rare moment of compassion.

"Um..." For a moment I'm not sure what pain she's talking about. Then she points at her own eye, indicating my shiner.

"It hurts," I say.

She hands me her joint again. I take another drag, because let's face it, it works.

"I can't believe none of the men asked about my bruises," I say.

"Your face isn't what they're looking at," she says.

I scowl at that, which hurts my face more. "But you would think…I mean…that one of them at least would report me as being beaten."

"Tommy don't usually chop his girls," she says. "You need to stay outta his cash."

Tommy comes back into the kitchen. "Nobody is reporting you to anybody," he says. He must have overhead what I said. "You're trash, Heather. A coke whore. The police ain't going to care."

He looks at Reg for support. She pulls out a kitchen chair and sits, taking a long toke of her joint. "He's right. They'll beat you worse," Reg says. "They don't care how or why you end up in jail. They're just going to lock you up and let you rot. A girl I know wound up in the slammer for possession of drugs. They beat her nearly senseless trying to get the name of her dealer."

"The cops aren't safe," Tommy says. "Not for people like you." He walks over to where I'm sitting and strokes the side of my cheek with his index finger. "You're *my* girl, Heather. I'm not going to let anybody hurt you." He twirls a strand of my hair between his fingers. I try not to pull away. I remember how he felt next to me that night he made love to me. He was different then. Softer.

I close my eyes and feel the drugs from Reg's joint lifting me up. The pain is going away.

"You love me, don't you?" Tommy says softly.

I nod. His hand is near my cheek, holding my hair, and I feel its warmth. My eyes are still closed, and for a moment I let myself believe that I'm safe.

Then Reg accidentally knocks her water bottle off the table and it lands with a bang on the cold, peeling linoleum. I jump. Tommy withdraws his hand and leans over to pick the bottle up. He sets it on the table and leaves us alone in the kitchen.

I decide then and there that if I want to escape, I'll need to get off of the drugs. I need a clear head. Between the pain in my face and the horror of my days (or nights?), I can't imagine going without them. But they cloud my judgment, so I decide that I will. I have to. If I'm going to get out of here, it's going to have to be of my own accord.

131

And so I get up and walk back towards the bedroom and undress. I climb under the blanket wearing only my underwear and a thin t-shirt. I'm so tired. And one final night, I let the drugs carry me off and away from the pain.

Tomorrow will be a new day.

— — —

I wake up the next morning with cramps. At first, it doesn't register with me, because I have grown so used to feeling awful. I always hurt "down there", and my stomach never feels good. Maybe it's the food. Maybe it's the fear. Or the drugs. I don't know. But when I go to the bathroom, I realize I've started my period.

A wave of relief washes over me. Now I can get the day off. The week off. I can crawl back into bed, hide under the covers, and sleep. Nobody will want to have sex with me now.

I look under the cabinet and find a box of pads. I grab one and put it on, then wash up and brush my teeth. I'm feeling a glimmer of hope.

I open the bathroom door, and Tommy is standing down the hall, arms crossed, having a conversation with one of his thugs, Sal. The thug is standing by the door, jangling his car keys. Tommy sees me looking at him.

"What's up?" he says.

"I can't work today."

Sal laughs.

Tommy cracks a smile. "And why not?"

I hesitate. I don't really want to announce it to a room full of guys.

"I..." I'm hoping Tommy will come closer so I can whisper it to him. But he remains where he is, so I have no choice. "I got my period today," I say quietly.

Sal starts to laugh, then turns to Thug Two and they leave the house, taking Serena with them. Tommy just smiles and tells me to go get dressed.

I stand there for a moment, unsure of what has just happened. Another cramp hits me, and I wonder if anybody has ibuprofen.

Reg comes out of our room, dressed for work.

"Do you have ibuprofen?" I ask.

She laughs. "In my dreams! Do you think they buy us that stuff?"

The cramps are getting bad, and I put my arms across my stomach.

"Cramps?" Reg says.

"Yes."

She shrugs and brushes past me. Chloe comes out of her room, having overheard us. "We don't get painkillers," she says.

I can't believe this. They all have illegal drugs that probably cost a fortune, but nobody has a bottle of ibuprofen?

"You need to get dressed," says Chloe. "Take an Oxy."

"I can't work today," I say. "I started my period."

Chloe frowns at me, as if she doesn't understand. "That don't matter," she says. "You still gotta work."

"But I can't. I'm having my period. You know...blood." This conversation seems unreal. Doesn't anybody get it? "No guy is going to pay for—"

But Chloe cuts me off. "There are other ways to please a man," she says quietly. "Figure it out. Tommy ain't going to give you no day off."

She gives me a small, encouraging smile, then heads off to the kitchen.

Seriously?

I always get a headache on the first day of my period, and I can feel one starting. It's throbbing behind my left temple. My stomach is cramping. And I feel just terrible.

Plus I am shaking. Withdrawal from the drugs, no doubt. Or maybe I'm just weak. I need more food.

"Heather? You about ready?" It's Tommy's voice coming from the kitchen. This is really happening. They really expect me to go do this.

I'm still sitting on my bed in my t-shirt when Tommy comes into the room. He grabs a dress out of the closet and throws it at me. It's one of Reg's, but I'm not going to tell him that. "Get dressed," he says. He stands there, arms crossed, and watches while I peel off the t-shirt and pull on the dress.

I don't bother with a bra. Then he tosses me a pair of heels out of the closet.

As he's leading me by the wrist to the car, I realize I've forgotten my baggie of pills. What if the pain gets too bad, and I need them? I remember that Chloe said to take an Oxy. Is that what those are? Maybe today isn't the best day to give up the drugs. Panic starts to set in.

"I can't," I say.

Tommy opens the back door of the car, and he pushes me in next to Chloe.

My mind is still spinning when we are suddenly at the hotel. There's a man waiting outside the door because we are a few minutes late.

He hands Tommy a $100-dollar bill, and Tommy pushes me towards him. And suddenly I'm inside the hotel room.

My heart is pounding, my head is pounding, my hands are shaking, and my stomach is cramping.

"I can't do this," I say to the stranger. "I'm sick."

"Sick?" the man says. He's dressed for work. Suit, tie, dress slacks. A businessman on his way into the office. Or on his lunch hour. He has a shiny gold ring on his wedding finger. "That doesn't matter. I have a good immune system."

"I mean…I got my period. I can't—"

"Shhhhh," he says, gently pushing me towards the bed. "It's okay. There are plenty of other ways to please me, and I'm sure you're good at all of them."

And that day, I find out what he means.

— — —

I grew up watching the old Disney movies. The princess was always in a predicament. Sleeping Beauty, Cinderella, Snow White. All of them needed saving, and their prince would come along and save them.

But then Mrs. Hudson told Brit and I that we shouldn't ever wait for a man to come and save us. We needed to be able to save ourselves.

So she made us watch *A League of Their Own*, about women who wanted to play professional baseball and started a team.

And *Erin Brockovich*, (even though it was rated R) where a woman takes on a legal case against a big company and wins. Then, thankfully, Disney got a clue and started making movies like *Mulan* and my favorite, *Frozen*, where the women save themselves and each other and sometimes an entire country. And we read the *Hunger Games*. So I'm well-equipped to realize that we women are capable of saving ourselves.

Except apparently *I'm not*.

Tommy's words ring in my ears. "You are pathetic, Heather. That's why you're here. You couldn't cope. You're not strong. This is all you're good for."

So maybe I do need a Prince Charming to come and save me.

I think of the movie *Pretty Woman*, where a prostitute meets a charming man and he falls in love with her. Maybe that will happen to me. Maybe, somehow, somebody will save me.

Chapter 29

Staying off drugs is harder than I thought it would be. First I'm sick and shaking and nauseated. Then I get cranky. Reg says it could be worse. I guess it could. It's not like I used them constantly. And I realize how much they were blocking my mind from what is happening to my body.

To distract myself, I spend the week looking for Prince Charming, but he never comes. So towards the end of that week I share my dreams with Chloe, who has only seen the early Disney movies. I can't believe you can grow up in America and not see *Mulan* or *Frozen*. I mean, was she hiding under a rock?

"You have to look out for yourself," Chloe says.

We're sitting in my bedroom. Reg, who is always high, and always grouchy, is lolling on her bed. Serena is there with us. It's a rare night when we are all at the house at the same time.

I have been here over a month, but the girls are just now telling me all the rules. Maybe because I'm just now ready to listen.

"The loose cash is kept in coffee containers under the kitchen sink," Chloe says. "Never touch them. Always ask Tommy. He will sometimes give you some to buy cigarettes or pads with. But never, ever take it. And never, ever, ever buy anything for yourself. He hates that." She wags her finger for emphasis. I nod.

"The food is whatever you can find in the kitchen. You haven't been here for long, but sometimes we run out. You just have to cope. Tommy always brings us more."

Reg smirks. "If you can call it food," she says, her voice gravelly.

136

Serena chimes in. I think I've only heard her speak a few times.

"He will sometimes give you drugs," she says. Her red hair is frizzy and framing her face in unorganized curls tonight. "Hang on to them if you can. You can sometimes sell them for cash for feminine products."

"Or condoms," Reg says and laughs.

She's making fun of me. She was right when she said the men won't wear them. I've never had one who would.

"What about…the pill?" I ask. This is something that has been scaring me. "I mean, can't we get pregnant?" Serena drops her head and starts picking at her nails.

"It has only happened to Serena," says Chloe. "Tommy took care of it."

"Took care of it?" I glance at Serena, who shrugs.

"It's no big deal." She picks at her nails some more and starts chewing on her thumb.

"You mean, abortion?" I say.

They are quiet, and for a moment I wonder if they actually have morals. If they *cared* about the baby. I can't imagine Reg caring for anyone but herself. Serena gets up and leaves, and Reg, true to form, dispels the myth of compassion.

"It nearly killed her," she says, her voice low. "Some abortion doc in the slums."

"I see. So they rape you, and then when you get pregnant, they nearly kill you to cover it up," I say, the anger getting to me.

"It's not really rape," Chloe says. "I mean, it's not like they're beating us."

I look at her so she can see my black eye. She's serious. I can't imagine in what world you have to grow up to think it's okay to do what men are doing to us.

"Are you kidding?" I say. Chloe shrugs. I look at Reg, who lights up another joint. The smoke is getting thick, and I feel a buzz from it. If I live long enough, I'll probably get lung cancer from second-hand smoke.

"You need to appreciate where you're at," Chloe says. "You could be out on the street, like I was. And Tommy gives us stuff." She pulls out a cigarette as if to prove a point. Then she lights it. Chloe just had her nails painted yesterday.

I think about Veronica back at my high school and wonder what happened to her. I hope she's okay. Did she ever return to school? Was she too ashamed, even though it wasn't her fault? Too embarrassed? And if she didn't return to school, will she still be able to get into college?

The more ways I play it in my head, the harder it is for me to figure out how Veronica could come back to finish up her senior year after that. I wonder what happened to the guys who did it to her. Are *they* in college?

It's almost like it's more shameful to be raped, than to be a rapist.

Maybe it was all too much for her. Maybe...maybe she killed herself.

— — —

I begin to wonder if suicide is my only way out. I could take an overdose of drugs. That would be easy enough. I think of the scars running down Reg's arms. They say when you slice all the way up your arms instead of across the veins, you mean business.

I could cut myself like that and then bleed to death. We have razors in the bathroom. I could do it at night, when nobody is looking. Maybe take some drugs to numb the pain in my arms. They wouldn't find me until it was too late.

But I don't want to die. I just want to go home.

I curl into a ball in my bed. Ha. When did I start thinking of this as *my bed*? I don't even know how long I've been here. Time is a blur, and I'm always tired. Always scared. Tommy doesn't keep a calendar around, and we aren't allowed cell phones. Sometimes when the television is on, I catch a date if it's a new show or something.

I just want to go home.

I bury myself deeper under my thin blanket, if that is even possible, and close my eyes tightly. I will myself to fall asleep, and because I am so exhausted, I do. Mercifully.

— — —

But all too soon Tommy is waking us up. I sit up groggily and get ready to face another day of horror. Reg isn't in the living room when we get there. She's taking her time in the shower. Chloe and I are alone.

"Don't talk to Reg this morning," Chloe whispers. "She's in a mood. She was arrested for drugs last night."

"What?" It never occurred to me that there are even police in this neighborhood. I haven't seen any ever. I would love to be arrested! Then I could tell them my story and escape.

"She was with a john, and they got pulled over. She was arrested for possession, but since it was the john's car, he's the one in trouble. I guess she quickly stashed it under the seat. Tommy bailed her out."

"Bailed her out?" I'm still having trouble wrapping my mind around this. This is our chance! The police! "Did she tell them where we are?"

"No!" Chloe hisses. We're still whispering so the men don't hear us. "Are you kidding? The police won't help you! You're just another whore selling yourself for drugs."

"Wait. What? No," I say. "That's not what's happening at all."

"That's what the police think. Don't get arrested, Heather. It'll be the end of you. If Tommy doesn't come to bail you out, they'll beat you. The police here— they're mean. They are our enemy. You're better off *here*."

It's a mantra they all keep repeating. I don't know how much of this is true, but now I'm really scared. If the local police can't help me, then who can?

Reg comes out of the bathroom dressed and made up. She looks exhausted, but she has her signature joint hanging out from between her lips.

"Let's go," she says.

And Tommy comes in to drive us to Hell.

Chapter 30

When I was in kindergarten, the police came to visit our school. We got posters to color that said "The Police are Our Friends," and all of us kids got plastic badges that looked just like the real thing. There were two officers, a woman officer who had red hair braided down her back, and a balding middle-aged man with kind eyes. I remember him the most. He's the same officer who later came to the house to tell me and my mom about Daddy's heart attack.

They taught us about Stranger Danger and how we could always count on them to help us.

"If you are lost, or scared, find a police officer and ask him or her for help," said our kindergarten teacher later that day. Mrs. Kettle was one of the nicest people I've ever known. Plump and grandmotherly, she made my start in school a good one. I loved going in each day to her class.

The police are our friends. I held that belief all through school. And I'm having trouble letting go of it now. If I ever see a police officer, I'm taking my chances.

When we get back to the house that evening, Chloe comes into my room, as usual, and sits on my bed. She brings me a glass of water and a pill of some sort.

"It'll help you sleep," she says. I put it on my bed.

"For later," I say. I don't want to hurt her feelings, but I also don't want to take it. I have no idea what's in it.

"I got arrested once," Chloe says. "So remember what I said this morning. Good night, Heather. Good night, Reg." She gives me a little smile, and leaves Reg and me in the dark.

Reg is lying in bed smoking a regular cigarette. I've gotten somewhat used to the smoke, and it doesn't quite give me a headache anymore. One of these days some of the hot ashes of whatever she's smoking are going to fall on the mattress, and we're all going to go up in flames. I just know it. And with the bars on the windows...

"Chloe has had it rough," Reg says. There's silence for a moment, then she continues. "I remember when *she* was arrested."

Reg doesn't usually speak to me, so I'm surprised that she is talking tonight. I turn over to face her.

"What happened?" I ask.

"It was last year. She was standing on the street corner doing her thing when she was picked up," Reg says. "Underage prostitution, they called it. They took her in, but Tommy showed up before they booked her. I don't know how he always knows where we are."

Reg takes another long drag of her cigarette. She's lying on her back, and when she exhales, I see the smoke drift up towards the ceiling and hang there like a dark cloud above her.

"So anyway, he got there and pretended to be angry at her."

"Pretended?"

Reg ignored that. "Said she was a runaway and that he'd take her home. The police said he needed to keep her off of the streets. She wasn't of age. And that was that."

I think about that. What officers would turn a fourteen-year-old girl back over to a guy like Tommy?

"That was it? Didn't they want to haul her off to foster care or something?"

"Chloe don't look her age," Reg said.

This is true. When she has her makeup and heels on, Chloe looks about 19. Maybe 20.

"And the police don't care," Reg says. "They called her a coke whore and a slut."

"I think I would try to escape," I said. But where would I go? No one was looking for me. They would have found me by now. And out there on the streets—if I try to escape on foot—the gangs will get me.

"We had another girl taken from us six months ago. Same thing. Arrested for underage prostitution. She wound up in a foster home."

This gave me a glimmer of hope. "What happened to her?"

"Tommy found her after school one day and brought her back. She's off in one of his other houses now."

"How many houses does he have? Are there other women like us?"

Reg shrugs and stabs her cigarette out. She rolls over so she is facing the wall, away from me.

"Reg?" I say.

But she doesn't answer. I take it that our conversation is over. I lay there for a long time, wondering about the girl who willingly came back to Tommy, and about young Chloe with her freshly painted fingernails. The world as I knew it no longer exists.

— — —

There's a photo in my dresser drawer at home of us as a family. It was taken on my ninth birthday, at the park where we had my birthday party. It was early June, and the weather was perfect that day. In the photo I'm wearing a pink shirt with kittens on it, and some polka dot shorts with a draw string. It was one of my favorite outfits. My hair is in braids and tied with pink bows. Mom has her brown hair pulled back in a ponytail and is wearing a Tigers' baseball cap. Daddy is wearing a light blue polo shirt that matches his eyes. It has green and yellow stripes through it, and even though he doesn't golf, Mom always called it his golf shirt. He looks so handsome in that photo, and his smile lights up his face. I still remember that. When Daddy smiled, his whole face smiled. Mom always said that about him. She said it was like his happy bubbled up from deep inside.

I have that picture memorized because I've looked at it so many times. It used to sit up on our fireplace mantel, but after Daddy died, Mom took it off because she said it made her too sad to look at. So I kept it. It's in my dresser drawer, and I look at it every night before bed. Or at least I used to, when I was home.

Mom made a baby photo book for me of my first year. We used to get it out every birthday and look through it together.

She had photos of my first bath, me eating my first solids, and pictures for each month of that first year of my life. There's also a little lock of hair in a protective sleeve, on a page titled first haircut. She said my bangs were so long she had to snip them. Near the end, she has photos of my very first birthday party. We were such a happy family.

I wonder what my mom is doing now. Is she looking for me? It seems like she's not. I think about how depressed she is, and how much she tried to get better both times for *me*.

"You're my inspiration," she said to me. "You're the reason I need to keep going."

But now that I'm gone, what is Mom's inspiration? This scares me. I think of Mom, all alone, with no idea how to find me. She takes more of her "feel good" pills to cope. One day she takes too many, and it's days before Brit's mom thinks to call. When Mom doesn't answer, Mrs. Hudson will go over and find her corpse, days old, rotting and alone.

My mom could be dead now. She has to be. Otherwise she would have found me and saved me.

— — —

Tommy takes us back out to the street corner. I don't have any drugs with me because I've run out. My hands are shaking, and I feel sick, but I am determined to break free of the haze they keep me in.

It's late evening, and we're picking up the after-work traffic. We spent a few hours in the hotel rooms first, but then Tommy said there was a change of plans. There is never an end to the stream of men who show up. I have no idea where they come from. Chloe has told me from ads. But some don't read the ads or go online. Instead, they cruise the streets of this bad part of town, looking for a way to satisfy their hunger. Which is why we're here now.

There's four of us today: me, Chloe, Serena and Reg. We're all here. I see two women standing a block down, and Chloe tells me that those are Tommy's girls, too. I can't tell much about them from here. I wonder if one is the girl who came back from foster care.

A car of two pulls up to our corner and stops. The guys look young, in their twenties. We usually get older men. Middle-aged men looking for something outside of their marriage. Or a way to relieve stress from their day at work. Or a way to satisfy a craving they didn't know they had.

They are all the same. But these two are different.

"Hey girls," says the guy in the passenger side. His hair is cut short and he has a tattoo on the right side of his neck of an eagle in flight. The wings are spread and wrap around towards the back of his neck. "Which one of you wants to have some fun?"

Reg saunters over to them and leans provocatively into his window. She blows some smoke into his face. "Do you think you can handle us?" she says.

The guy blushes a bit and coughs, but he regains himself. "Oh baby, you know we got what it takes." He reaches his hand down, and I can't see, but he probably grabs his crotch.

Reg gives him a smirk and stands back up. "What about you, handsome?" she says to the man driving the car.

"There's only one way to find out," he says, grinning.

"Which one of my sisters do you want to join us?"

They look at us, their eyes scanning our bodies like we're meat.

"That one," the driver says, and he's pointing at Chloe.

Reg nods and opens the back door of the car. Chloe gets in, and Reg is about to.

"No," says the passenger. "Just her."

Reg freezes. I see her shoulders go stiff. "We come in pairs," she says. "Two guys means two girls, twice the fun."

"No," says the passenger. He has grown some balls and gets out of the car. "Just her." He pushes the back door shut and stands against it, folding his arms across his chest. "I'm sure you're hot, but we're not looking for your type this evening."

Reg's eyes dart across the street, and I follow her gaze. One of Tommy's thugs is standing there, arms folded, watching.

Chloe has seen Thug One as well. "I'll be fine," she says.

Reg steps back and gives her signature shrug. "Have it your way," she says to the blond guy. He nods, giving her a smile. I can see the bulge in his pants from here. He gets back into the car and closes the door. They drive off.

"Rookies," says Reg.

"You mean...virgins?" I ask.

"Or at least they've never paid for it before," she says. She takes a long drag of her joint. Her fingers are trembling. I don't often see Reg upset. She tries to look like she doesn't care, but she looks scared to me.

"What will happen to Chloe?" I ask.

Reg shrugs.

"They'll kill her," Serena says. I jump at her voice. She's quiet and hardly ever speaks, so I forget she's there.

"Shut up," Reg says. "Chloe can take care of herself."

"But two guys..."

"She's had more." Reg walks away from us, sauntering down the street. Another car slows down, and she leans in. Soon she is sliding in the passenger side and closing the door. They drive away.

I can't help but think of what Serena just said.

"How do you know they'll kill Chloe?" I said.

"They have that look. They're too eager. Some men are not just here for sex. They're here to *prove* something. Sometimes the younger ones need to prove they're men, and that usually makes them mean."

I look across the street at Thug One. "Should we tell him?"

Serena shakes her head. "He doesn't care."

"Tommy might."

But she doesn't reply. I wonder again what Serena's story is. She never talks about herself, and the other girls don't seem to know, either. She's pretty, she speaks well, and she seems educated. I wonder if she was like me. Foolish enough to be lured in.

A pickup truck pulls up, and a man rolls down his window. I hear country music playing from his stereo. "You." He points to me. He waves some cash. "Let's go."

I glance across the street and see Thug One still standing there. Then I turn to Serena. "I'll see you at home," I say.

She nods as I climb in the truck. The man puts his hand on my thigh and runs it up between my legs. I flinch at his touch. I can't help myself. He holds his hand there as he begins to drive. He is wearing jeans and a cowboy hat. His leather boots say he has money.

As we drive off it occurs to me that when I said goodbye to Serena, I told her I'd see her tonight at home.

Home.

Is that what I'm calling it now?

Chapter 31

When I get back to the house sometime in the wee hours of the morning, I hear Serena in her bedroom crying. Instead of heading to the kitchen for some food, I turn and go into her room.

Reg is sitting on Chloe's bed, smoking. She looks at me then nods towards Serena. "Chloe is at the hospital," she says. "She was beaten pretty badly. Tommy went to get her."

"Oh no." I think of Chloe's sweet face. And of the two men who picked her up.

"I knew they were trouble," says Reg. "They had her for a while before Sal found her. She was in an alley, bleeding all over some garbage."

"Is she...will she be okay?" I suddenly feel light-headed and sit on the bed next to Serena.

Reg shrugs. Sometimes when she does that I want to hit her.

"What else do you know?"

"That's about it. That and Tommy went nuclear when he found out," Reg said.

I sit with Serena for about an hour, until the dizziness is too much. Then I go in search of some food. I find a microwave meal in the freezer, a welcome treat from the usual frozen burrito or pizza pocket. It's beef and noodles. I put it in the microwave and then think of Serena. I get a glass of water and go back to Serena's room. She is still sitting on her bed crying. Reg is gone.

"Do you want some food?" I ask gently.

Serena shakes her head no. I set the glass of water down on the floor near her feet in case she wants it later.

I go into the kitchen, eat my meal, and drink three glasses of water. Then I sit there, thinking about Chloe until Tommy comes in. He looks tired.

"They're keeping her a few more hours," he says. "I can go back to get her later this morning."

I nod. The fact that Chloe is coming back to us gives me a rare feeling of comfort. I realize then that I have grown to love her, in a way.

The food is making me sleepy, and out our little kitchen window I see the morning sky lightening up on the horizon. I make my way down the hall and find Reg sleeping, her arms wrapped around her pillow. I fall into bed without changing clothes or showering.

And I dream of myself when I was young.

In the dream I'm about seven. Brit and I are on the school playground. Chloe comes to our school as the new girl, and she is little, maybe only five. She has started kindergarten with my favorite teacher, Mrs. Kettle. We invite Chloe to play, and I'm happy, because in kindergarten you learn that the police are your friends, and this time, maybe, the balding man with kind eyes will save Chloe. Save her before it's too late.

When I wake up, the analog clock on our dresser reads that it's after noon, and Tommy hasn't come for us yet. I sit up and rub my eyes, and right away the gnawing sensation of fear starts in on me.

With a start, I remember Chloe. I look over at the other bed, and Reg is there, staring at the ceiling. No cigarette. No makeup. Just lying there staring.

"Did you hear Chloe come in?" I ask.

"Yeah. She looks terrible. Prepare yourself." Then she abruptly gets up, tossing her blanket on the floor. "I have to pee."

As Reg leaves, I part the window curtain near my bed and see that it's a gray day outside. If Chloe is back, she must be okay. At least okay enough for the hospital to release her.

I pull on some jeans and tiptoe quietly down the hall to her room. I always try to avoid the men. I don't see anybody, but I hear Tommy's voice talking quietly to someone in the kitchen. Chloe's bedroom door is closed, and I open it quietly, trying not to make any noise.

She's laying in her bed, her back to me.

I tiptoe in.

"Chloe?" I whisper.

"Heather?" Her voice sounds normal enough, but I still can't see her face.

"Oh Chloe, I'm *so glad* you're okay!"

She slowly turns over, and I'm so horrified when I see her face that I take a step back. Her right eye is purple and swollen shut. Her lips are swollen and caked with blood. And I see scratch marks down her arms, as if an animal has attacked her.

"What on earth....?" I say, but she quickly pulls the covers up over her.

"Nothing's broken," she says, giving me a crooked little smile through swollen lips. "Tommy says I was lucky."

"Were you at...I mean...the hospital let you *come home?*"

"Yeah. They're busy and short of beds. It's okay."

"You need to let somebody know what happened!" I say, my voice raising above a whisper. "Did you tell one of the nurses?"

"Shhhh!" says Chloe. She glances at the other bed, and I see that Serena is still asleep. "You'll wake her. She was up all night waiting for me."

"Was it those two guys? Did they just hit your face?" I asked. "Or...or are your hurt everywhere?" I have to know.

"I needed stitches," Chloe says.

"Did they cut you?" I imagine knives and stab wounds on petite little Chloe. "Where?"

Chloe shakes her head. "No. No cutting. Just..." her voice trails off. "They were a little rough. With the sex and all. You know how it goes."

It takes a moment to sink in, but from my own experience I get what she's saying. "You mean you have stitches...*down there?*"

Chloe nods. "I tore."

"Oh my gosh." Suddenly the room tips, and I sit down on the side of her bed. They raped her so badly she tore. I have no words of comfort. There is nothing I can even think to say. I can't even imagine. I feel tears in my eyes, but when I turn to Chloe, her eyes are dry.

She puts a hand on my wrist. I see the scratch marks on her arms again. "It's okay," she says.

"No, it's not," I say. I'm crying now.

"It is. Tommy will take care of me. He gave me some aspirin. I'll be fine." She lets go of my arm. "But I need to get some sleep."

I nod, taking the clue from her to leave. Then I stand and walk towards the door. I'm about to close it quietly behind me when Tommy comes down the hall and pushes past me.

"Serena, get up. Heather? Why aren't you girls dressed? Chloe stays home, the rest of you have work!" He's bellowing, even though we're right there. I shrink back from his loud voice, and hurry to my room. I hope he takes us straight to the hotels today. Now, after what happened to Chloe, I'm more afraid than ever to work the streets.

Back in my room, Reg is dressed and putting on mascara. She tosses a baggie with two white pills in it on my bed.

"Those are free," she says. "Because of what happened to Chloe, I thought maybe you could use something to settle your nerves."

She doesn't look at me.

"Thanks," I say. I put my bra on and stuff them down in. I know I gave up drugs, but I take them with me anyway. I just may need them today.

"Why did the hospital let her go?" I ask.

"It's an inner city dump," says Reg. "She was just another whore who got beat up by her John. They see it every day. She's eighteen, so legally they have to let her go if she asks."

"She's not eighteen," I say.

"She is on paper."

It hasn't occurred to me that some of the girls might have fake ID. I feel so stupid. "But isn't anybody looking for her? I mean, whoever she was stolen from in the first place? Or a foster home? Or *somebody*? Wouldn't they recognize her by her description?"

"There are so many girls who have gone missing. Do you think the people in the ER have time to look at every missing photo that comes through? And besides, nobody is looking for her. She ain't got nobody. Tommy found her on the streets, alone and starving. Chloe isn't even her real name."

"What *is* her real name?"

Reg shrugs. "I'm not even sure she knows."

"How can she not know her name?"

But Reg is done talking. She finishes putting on her makeup and heads out the door. I hurry up, too, because if I'm late, Tommy will be mad. And with the mood he's in today, I don't want to face him angrier.

How can someone not know their own name?

———

Heather was the name of my great-grandmother on Daddy's side. His mom's mom. Because his mom lived only three streets over from her parents, she spent a lot of time at their house when Daddy was little. He had fond memories of baking cookies and coloring with his Grandma Heather. Later, when Daddy showed an interest in painting, it was Grandma Heather who bought him his first watercolor paints. She took him to an actual art store to buy nice paper and expensive brushes, even though he was only about ten years old.

But Grandma Heather was more than sweet and fun. She stood up for what she believed in. Born in 1923, my great-grandma Heather saw her brothers go off to war, and she went to work as a teenager for the war effort. When she turned eighteen, she took college classes locally. Then, not to be held back by her gender, she enrolled in Harvard in 1945, the year the first females were accepted into the prestigious medical program. She had a heart for war veterans and decided she could help them more with a medical degree. She became a physician assistant and worked part time for nearly twenty years in the local veterans' hospital.

In the 1960s she marched for Martin Luther King and burned her bra for Women's Rights. In the 1970s she volunteered with helping returning Vietnam veterans get jobs. Because she was also a part-time stay-at-home mom, once her kids were older and in school, she had time to volunteer with the local food bank, the elementary school down the street, and the library. She doted on her kids and later her grandkids. Daddy told me countless stories of everything that Grandma Heather did, and how much everybody loved her.

She died tragically when Daddy was a freshman in college. She was crossing a street on her way to the local food bank to volunteer her time serving soup, when someone ran a red light and hit her at the crosswalk. Daddy said at least she died doing something she loved doing.

Kind of like Daddy.

He was grief-stricken, and he met my mom six months later. They fell in love quickly, and he said if they ever married and had kids, he wanted to name their daughter Heather. Mom loved the idea, so when I was born, I was given Grandma Heather's name.

I have a photo of Grandma Heather in my room. She's in her fifties in the photo and has long dark hair, like mine, and my same brown eyes. I have always loved my name because of her.

And my middle name is Jean, from my mom. That's her name, although Daddy always called her Jeanie.

I wonder what Chloe's name is, and if she ever had a family who loved her enough to give her a special one. There's a lot in a name.

Chapter 32

I hate leaving Chloe behind, but Tommy drops me off at the motel. The first guy comes in, and he's quick.

When I'm with the men, I've found a way to pretend I'm somewhere else. I close my eyes and go as far away from myself as I can. Sometimes I pretend I am home playing with Gracie, and she's purring. I try to make the purring so loud in my head that I can't hear the men grunting.

Sometimes I pretend that I'm on my way to Brit's house, and I'm driving in my car. I turn the music up really loud in my head so I can't hear or feel anything else. Just the beat of the music.

But mostly, I just go away. I go away someplace empty and don't hear or see or feel. I just get through the day.

It's hard without the drugs. The monotony of it, the pain of it, the disgusting smells and touching and fluids and sweat become too much for me.

Dark thoughts start entering my mind. That's been happening a lot lately, but today I think of Chloe, lying home in bed, in pain. Torn. Bleeding. I wonder when Tommy will make her work again. Will he give her time to heal? Probably not completely.

I think of Reg and the long cuts up her arms. I wonder when she tried to kill herself. And who stopped her? Who found her and rushed her to the hospital? I'll have to ask Chloe.

There's a man on top of me, and he's huffing and pushing, and his sweat is sliding across my stomach and dripping down my sides. He stinks. The low light from the small lamp doesn't hide the hairs in his ears, which I can see clearly because the side of his head is up against my eyes, rocking back and forth.

I feel bile creeping up in my throat, and just as he empties himself in me, I turn over, spilling him out and vomiting over the side of the bed. There's not much in my stomach, just a candy bar this morning and one glass of water, so my vomiting soon turns to dry heaves.

I hear him exclaiming something, then cursing. He gets up and throws the covers over me, muttering something about how disgusting I am, but I am clinging to the sides of the bed, heaving up air and noise, and nothing else.

I hear the rustle of clothes. The zip of his pants. And then, the slam of the door.

I hope he left the money.

I hang over the side of the bed for a few minutes, until the heaving stops. Then I roll back over. I'm naked and covered in sweat and filth, and his sperm has leaked across my thighs, and all I can think of is how much I don't ever want to do this again.

Where is my mom?

Why did Daddy die and leave me?

Why hasn't Brittney come to save me?

In the Disney movies, the later ones, the princesses are always saving themselves. And the world. Or their friends. Or their pets. *Somebody*. And in *Hunger Games* Katniss saves herself. And Peta.

And in the beginning, her sister.

But me? I can't even keep myself from getting raped.

And what did I do for Chloe? I shouldn't have let her go with those men. I should have stopped her.

The door is opening and the next guy is coming in. How long have I lain here? He sees the pile of vomit on the floor and steps over it.

He takes his pants off and I see him growing inside of his briefs.

I close my eyes and retreat back into the world of nothingness.

— — —

The watery vomit soaks into the dirty carpeting and stays there the rest of the night. People just step over it, or don't notice it. I am too tired and depleted to clean it up. My hands are shaking because I'm so hungry. I only ate the candy bar, and I can't remember the last time I drank water, but apparently it was long ago because I haven't had to pee all day.

I can't quit thinking about Chloe.

It's late. Or early morning. The clock in the hotel says 2:30 a.m. I'm waiting for another man to come in. This one is late, I guess, because I have had some time in between clients. I fell asleep briefly, and I am chilled. I feel feverish. Maybe I'm sick. But then in the back of my head, I remember learning in Health Class that if you are dehydrated, you can feel feverish. I really should go get myself a drink of water.

I sit up, and the room spins. I take a few deep breaths, and when the dizziness recedes I walk naked to the bathroom and fill up one of the glass cups on the sink.

I drink it all.

I feel really light-headed, so I fill it up again and take it back to the bed. I'm about to sit down when I see my bra laying on the floor near my dress. It has the package of white pills near it.

I pick up the baggie and hold it between my fingers. What if I take one, just to knock the edge off?

I open the baggie and swallow one before I have time to talk myself out of it.

Chloe's face comes back into my head. Her big eyes, so wide and pretty; one now swollen shut. Her lips caked with blood. I see a picture of those guys who picked her up so vividly in my mind, of them beating her, of them both raping her. And her alone in a motel room with no one to help her.

I take another pill. I wash it down with the water.

I don't ever want to be like Chloe. I don't want to be like Reg and slit my wrists. I don't want Tommy to hit me again, or for another man to lay on top of me and use me to make himself feel better.

I want to go away. Farther away than I go in my head when the men are here. Farther away than back home, or out of this town.

I want to see Daddy again. And meet Grandma Heather. And laugh and be safe. I want to go somewhere where no one can hurt me again.

I swallow a third pill and drink the last of the water. Then I lay down on the bed and wait for rest to come.

— — —

"What the—?" Someone is standing over me, cursing. Through slit eyes I see it's a man. He has a beard, and he's white. His beard is black. He's black and white.

"Hey," he says. He slaps me gently on the cheek. I moan but can't talk. I turn my head, and he pats me on the other cheek. "Hey. You okay?"

I want to tell him to leave. To let me go away. But I can't speak.

I can't even keep my eyes open.

"Are you sick?" His voice raises a pitch. "Did you OD?"

He is starting to freak out. I hear him jangling his car keys, fishing through his pants pocket. Then he has his phone out and is punching buttons.

I hear Grandma Heather talking to me. She's telling me to come home. In my mind, I am running towards her, and I am a child again, and there's flowers in the field I'm crossing. Flowers of light blue and lavender. And then just as I'm about to reach her, blackness closes in on me.

— — —

Bright lights. There's a terrible pain in my stomach. A tube down my throat. A gurgling sound.

"Here it comes," says someone. I squint up at the lights and see someone wearing a green cap. It looks like a nurse. The gurgling becomes louder, and I fade out again.

— — —

156

I open my eyes, and I'm in a bed. There's a needle in my arm and a bag of something dripping down a tube to my veins. Someone put an IV in. Tommy is standing by my bed.

"You really messed up this time," he says to me. His arms are crossed. He's wearing the look he has when he's not happy.

I turn my head a little bit. It looks like I'm in a hospital. An emergency room, maybe, because there's a curtain separating the beds.

I try to sit, but I'm really light-headed.

"Lie still," Tommy says. "You need a few more fluids, and then you can go."

I lie back and do as he says. I'm really groggy, but as soon as a doctor comes, it's my chance to get out of here. I try to fight through the fog in my head to find the right words. Help. Rape. Hostage.

I drift off again and...

"Coke whore," someone is saying quietly. "They sell themselves for drugs. That's what they all do. This one overdosed."

The whispered voices are coming from behind the curtain. A man and a woman. The curtain is pulled aside, and they both come in. To my left I see Tommy sitting in a chair next to my bed.

"Got your stomach pumped," the nurse says. She is older than my mom, and her hair is grey. She has frown lines all over her face. She looks down at me and shakes her head but doesn't make eye contact.

The doctor, a middle-aged white man with bags under his eyes, looks at the monitors overhead and pulls out my chart.

"She's good to go," he says. "We need the space. There was a gang fight, and we have several coming in." He hands Tommy something to sign.

I don't want to be here but can't say that because Tommy is still here. What if they don't believe me and send me home with him? He'll kill me. And I have to take care of Chloe.

The doctor takes the signed clipboard from Tommy and abruptly leaves. He's gone before I can think of what to say.

The nurse is pulling out my IV. I hear a lot of noise on the other side of the room. People are shouting. Someone is crying.

"I…" I begin. My voice isn't working. My brain is all foggy.

In a last-ditch effort to communicate, I reach for the nurse's arm, but she's gone.

"Let's go," Tommy says. I sit up, and he throws my clothes at me. He pulls the curtain closed but stays while I change out of the hospital gown and back into the skimpy dress. My fingers are weak and fumbling with things, so I don't bother with the fishnet stockings. And I decide to carry the heels instead of wearing them.

I stand on shaky legs, and Tommy takes my arm. He leads me down the aisleway, where there are beds of sick or injured people on both sides. Past drugged up people— past gang members wearing colors, who are standing and bleeding from what looks like stab wounds, past a black woman who is screaming, her hair all wild. And past a howling baby.

The doctors and nurses all have dark circles around their eyes, grim faces, and an aura of exhaustion around them. Their patients, people who have seen a harder side of life than I ever had, wait to be helped. Some of them are angry; most of them look hopeless. They are tended to in an almost mechanical way born from familiarity and exhaustion.

Tommy's right. Nobody here cares.

Chapter 33

The first time I was in an emergency room was for my mom. Mrs. Hudson had gone over to visit and found her collapsed on the floor. She called an ambulance, and they took her in, declaring an overdose. But Mom hadn't tried to kill herself. She had simply gotten some bad meds.

I was fifteen and was in school when this happened. I knew something was up when Mr. Hudson picked me up from school with Brit instead of letting me ride the bus home that afternoon. "Your mom is sick," he said. "She's at the hospital with Brittney's mom. She's going to be okay."

Of course, I wanted to know everything, but he would only give me sketchy details. She fell. She had a reaction to some medication. She is tired and needs some rest. They will keep her overnight.

I wanted to see her. When we got back to my house, I put my backpack down on the kitchen table and turned to him. "She's the only family I have," I said, tears springing to my eyes. "You can't keep her from me. You can't!!"

"It's not fair, Daddy," Brit said. "You need to take her."

Gracie came to greet me, and realizing I was upset, started meowing loudly. I picked her up and hugged her to me. "You can't keep me from my mother. I'll call a taxi. I'll get to the hospital one way or another. So you might as well drive me."

I could see that I was wearing him down. I felt kind of bad, because I loved him like a father, but at that moment, I didn't care if I was upsetting him. I wanted to see my mom. I had already lost one parent, and I was scared to death I'd lose them both.

Finally he sighed and nodded. "Okay," he said. "Get in the car."

On the way we dropped Brit off at home because she had a lot of homework and they needed her to watch her little brother when he got home from school. His elementary bus came later than ours. Mr. Hudson ran inside and grabbed me a granola bar and a grape juice box. When I popped the straw in the top of the juice box, some of the purple juice spilled out on my white t-shirt. I tried to dab it off with the napkin he handed me, but it soaked in. I ate the bar and drank in the car on the way to the hospital.

They had Mom in a room when I got there. Apparently, Mrs. Hudson had found her this morning right after school started. Nobody had bothered to tell me because "they didn't want to scare me, and there was nothing I could do." Of course, there was something I could do! I could be here with her!

When we walked in, Mrs. Hudson shot a look at Mr. Hudson, and I saw him shrug. He was going to be in trouble later for bringing me in. I didn't care.

Mom was dressed in a hospital gown and hooked up to an IV. She lay in her bed with the head slightly raised. Her hair was wild, the brown strands flying loosely around and staticky from the dry air in the room.

"Heather!" she said and attempted a smile. She had dark bags under her eyes, and her skin was grey. I wondered how long she had looked like this. Had I not noticed?

"What's wrong?" I asked her. But it was Mrs. Hudson who answered.

"She's having a reaction to some medication she took," Mrs. Hudson said.

Mom's hands were shaking a lot. Her breathing was coming in short gasps. She was sweating.

I turned to Mrs. Hudson. I was really scared. "Is she going to be okay?" I asked. My voice trembled a little bit.

"Yes," Mrs. Hudson said. She pulled me towards her and hugged me to her chest. I let her. She was warm and vaguely smelled of the jasmine candle she kept in her living room. "She is. But it will take some time."

I wasn't so sure about that. Mom looked worse than I have ever seen her.

They didn't let me stay with Mom for very long. And Mom didn't seem to mind when I left. She was concentrating on survival. I didn't know it then, but she was starting to go through withdrawal symptoms from the drugs she had been on.

Mr. Hudson drove me home to get my things and feed Gracie. Then I spent the night with them, and I ended up staying there while Mom went through in-patient rehab. It was a long two weeks. When she was healthy enough to come home, I couldn't have been happier. She cleaned up her act and worked hard to get better. I had no idea that that was just the beginning of her descent.

— — —

Tommy stops the car, and I open my eyes. He let me ride in the front seat this time. We are parked in the driveway of our house.

"How did I get to the hospital?" I ask.

"The man you were with called 911," Tommy says. Then he swears some and sits back in the driver's seat, crossing his arms. "There I am, driving around, and I see an ambulance at your motel room. The door wide open. People working on you. So of course, I stopped in to check on you. To see what happened. Do you have *any idea* how embarrassing that was for me? That one of our clients had to find you like that? That's a customer we'll never see again," Tommy says. "You're just lucky he cared, or you'd be dead."

I think about that. Was that guy showing compassion or trying to keep himself out of trouble? "What happened to him?" I ask.

"He ran," Tommy said. "He was nowhere in sight when the ambulance got there. Or when I got there. You think he's gonna stick around and wait for the police?"

I guess not. He *was* paying for sex. And probably married.

"I just thought the police would have let him off, you know, since he saved me."

Tommy looked over at me. "The police aren't your friends, Heather. How many times do I have to beat that into your stupid head? And the hospital staff isn't, either. You see how you were treated. You're barely able to walk, and they throw you out. You're worthless. They prefer to spend their time and energy on the important people."

Not a "coke whore." The doctor's words swirl through my head.

"Nobody cares about you," Tommy adds for emphasis. "Nobody." Then he turns towards me so he is facing me. "Except for *me*. I give you food and a bedroom, a bed to sleep in. Toiletries. A house to live in." His voice turns tender. "You know I love you, right?"

When I don't answer, he reaches his hand over and gently takes my chin. He turns my head so I have to look at him. I meet his brown eyes with my green ones.

"Right?" he says again. "You know that I love you?"

I swallow, and then nod. Because it's what he wants to hear. And because maybe, in some way, he does. He *did* come to save me. To bring me home.

He lets go of my chin and turns to face the front of the car again. "I'm in a tight spot right now, Heather," he says. "Chloe is unable to work for a few more days. And here you are. A risk. If something happens to you, I won't have the income to pay the bills and buy groceries for the other girls. I can't have you overdosing again. Drugs aren't something you can just play around with."

"I know." My head is hurting, and I wish he would quit talking. I just want to go inside and crawl into bed. And sleep. The sky is light, and his dashboard clock says 8:12 a.m.

"So, here's what we're going to do. No more drugs for you. Not until I'm sure you're mature enough to handle them."

I nod. I just want to go inside.

He turns to me. Waits until I look him in the eye. "Okay?" he says again.

"Okay," I say. And finally, he takes the keys out of the ignition and walks me into the house.

Chapter 34

The days all blur together, and schedules don't exist anymore. I used to be able to break the weeks up by the weekends, but we don't ever get a day off, so I'm not always sure when a week begins or ends.

But several of them pass. Over time, Chloe heals, at least outwardly. Nothing else changes. Reg, Serena and I continue to be pressed into daily routines. The weeks turn into months. I can tell by the way the seasons change. We went through summer and into fall. I can tell because the days are colder again and because of the dry, brown weeds and grass I see through the cracks in the sidewalk and our scrawny lawn. I miss the brilliant yellow of our maple tree back home. It sits in our front yard, welcoming me home from school every day in the fall like a beacon.

There's no beauty in this world. None.

I've started my period, and there are only two sanitary pads left in the house. Tommy let me start having drugs again a few months ago, and I've saved them. Lucky for me, one of the John's I have that day is willing to pay for a joint, so I ask Thug One to stop at a corner pharmacy on the way home so I can buy some pads. Chloe told me about this store. Before, I've always relied on the other girls or Tommy to supply what we needed. Sometimes if we run out of toilet paper or soap, one of the other girls will buy some. A few times Chloe manages to smuggle us in some cookies from some place. We never ask where it comes from. Or how they paid for it. We just accept the gifts and try to enjoy them. But this time I was desperate, so I asked Chloe where I could buy some necessities.

The store is cluttered, and one of the fluorescent lights is flickering. The man behind the counter is old and pot-bellied. He has a television station turned on but muted. It's some sports program with boxing. There are a lot of unsavory characters, and one man who is there buying beer leers at me. He has tattoos up both his arms, but I don't look closely. I avoid eye contact with everyone most of the time.

In this part of town it's one of the only stores open, and I'm pretty sure it's also a front for something else. Chloe told me once that it's a good place to buy drugs, but I've never tried.

I glance up, and there are no security cameras anywhere that I can see. I always have a small hope that someone, somewhere, will recognize me. I'm certain Brit has put ads out about my disappearance. But it has been almost a year. Can they still be looking? I'm not even sure my mom is alive.

I push those thoughts aside and make my way to the back of the store, where I find some boxes of feminine pads. There's a thin line of dust across the tops of them. I pick up a box. With the money I have hidden in my bra, I think about buying some ibuprofen for my cramps. So I head to the painkiller section. The boxes are faded. I look at the dates stamped on them. All of them expired at least three years ago. I grab a box anyway. I guess people don't really buy stuff here anymore.

Except beer. The man who leered at me is at the counter. He pays for his beer and steps back. I set the box down on the counter and hear him snicker.

"You working tonight?" he says.

I ignore him and pay. It's not really 'night' anyway. It's some wee hour of the morning. Idiot.

The balding man is slow and rings up my order. He keeps glancing up at the television. I notice a calendar sitting by the register. Today is February 2nd. Groundhog Day. I have been here for eleven months.

"I was talking to you," the leering man behind me says.

I continue to ignore him. But then I get my change and have to turn around so I can leave. He's standing there, blocking my way.

"Heather, right?

Startled that he knows my name, I finally look at him. And I recognize him. He has been with me a few times.

I can't stop the flush that comes to my cheeks. The anger, the shame. I want to pound him in the face, but he's twice my size.

"Excuse me," I say, and try to brush past him, but he steps in front of me again, blocking my way.

I glance at the guy behind the cash register. He is concentrating on scraping some dirt out from underneath his fingernail, not wanting to get involved.

I look leering guy in the eye and try to glare. I'm trying to act tough, but my hands are shaking. I put them behind my back. "Move," I say, my voice firm.

He smiles, and I can see his black teeth. "Because if you're working tonight, I'll see you later," he says.

"I'm done," I say.

"Well, tomorrow then," he says. With the hand that's not holding the beer, he reaches up and twirls a strand of my hair around his fingers, then lets it fall. I cringe.

He blows me a kiss and steps out of my way.

I walk as quickly as I can back outside and to the car, my only point of safety at the moment. I'm relieved to see that Thug One has it waiting at the curb, still running. I climb in the back seat and he starts driving. As we head back towards the house, I exhale. Relieved. But for how long?

As we drive home, I begin to feel really depressed. Here I am, eleven months into a life of hell. I can't escape. I can't fight off any of these men. The only friend I have in the world is Chloe, and who's to say she wouldn't turn on me in a minute? I know Reg would. And probably Serena. I haven't seen any other women, except when they are standing on a street corner or walking into a hotel room. Tommy doesn't like for us to mix.

At home I wash two ibuprofens down with a glass of water and eat a package of cheese and crackers. Then I go to the bathroom to wash up. I hardly recognize myself these days. There are dark circles under my eyes, and I'm pale without my makeup. My hair is thin and stringy. And I'm skinny.

Without my clothes on, I can count my ribs and see my collar bones standing up.

Suddenly, I feel really, really tired. I've spent the past eleven months – *eleven months* – trying to think of a way to escape. Hoping for rescue. Wanting to be free.

There's a knock on the bathroom door. "Heather?"

It's Chloe.

"I have to pee."

I finish up and dress for bed, pulling on fresh underwear and a ratty t-shirt. When I open the door, there is Chloe, made up to look ten years older than she is. She gives me a big smile.

"All done," I say, and brush past her.

A little while later, while I'm curled up in my bed, she quietly comes in and sits next to me.

"What's wrong?" she says quietly. Reg is already asleep, and we can hear her softly snoring.

"What isn't?" I say bitterly.

"But you look different today. Sadder than usual."

I sigh and sit up, pulling the blanket around me. It's cold in here, and I'm thinking of putting my jeans on and another shirt to sleep in. I do that sometimes when I can't get warm. Tommy won't give us more blankets. He says he can't afford such luxuries unless we work harder. And none of us are willing to do that, so we don't complain.

"It's just..." I look at her. She has washed her makeup off and looks so young again. Her face is still beautiful, not full of scars or tattooed like some of the other girls. She's Tommy's pride. His most beautiful girl. He hopes to keep her that way.

"It's just that I'm such a loser," I say, and with those words my whole life seems suddenly summed up. The words begin to spill out. "My dad died when I was ten, and I wasn't enough for my mom. I just couldn't be enough to fill the hole Daddy left, and she broke from her grief. She needed drugs to escape life—life with *me*. So I thought I'd work really *really* hard in school and get good grades. Then I could get into a great university and become a doctor. Make lots of money, you know?"

Chloe nods.

"But I couldn't even do *that*. I'm too stupid."

I pull the thin blanket tighter around myself. I'm starting to cry.

"And I stayed away from boys, and dating, because I didn't want to get distracted from my studying. No boys, no drama, right? I was a virgin before…" I spread my arms wide indicating the room, "before all of this."

Chloe's eyes get wide. "Really?"

"Yes. I was. And I was okay with that. And with not dating. But then I met Cory."

I feel a lump form in my throat. Despite all that he did to me, despite all the trouble he caused me, I still feel so sad when I think about him. About the dream that I thought was, and about who he *really* was instead. What a fool I was. What a fool.

"Cory," Chloe says. "Tell me about him."

I start with how he came into my coffee shop and was so handsome, with that golden hair and blue eyes, his shy smile. And later, his hot car. And how he seemed really interested in me, and how we had so much in common.

"Sounds nice," Chloe says.

I give a short laugh. "Yeah, but he was only using me."

I tell her how he took me to his "dad's" house, and then how he brought me here. "To sell me. He dropped me like I was trash," I say. "He never felt anything for me. To him I was just…I don't know. A way to make money?"

"He was so mean to you," Chloe says.

I nod and realize I'm crying harder. Silent tears are running down my face. I wipe them away with a corner of the blanket.

"But Tommy's not like that," Chloe says. "Now that you're here, he'll take care of you."

I look up at her. Her wide eyes and pale, round face. She'll never get it. She doesn't know what I was like "before." She will never understand, because she never had a "before." At least not a good one. Her "before" was worse than her "now."

"Yeah," I say quietly. "You're right." I wipe my nose on the blanket and pat her on the arm. "Go get some sleep, Chloe. Tomorrow isn't far away."

She leans forward and gives me a little hug, then turns to go. As I watch her small frame disappear through my door, I vow to myself that if I ever do get out of here, I'll come back for her. Chloe will have a chance to know a different life. I won't let her down.

Chapter 35

"I'll always be here for you," Brit said.

We were sitting on the playground swings, licking our ice cream cones. It was summer, we were sixteen, and Aaron was working at the local custard shop. He always gave us extra custard when we bought cones. Today we both had chocolate. It was *so* rich and creamy! The day had been a record-setting hot one, and the evening was one of those warm summer evenings where the air is the same temperature as your skin so you can't really "feel" the air. I remember how cool the dessert felt on my tongue.

When I didn't answer, Brit said it again.

"Heather." She waited until I looked at her. "I'll *always* be here for you."

"You will?" I said. My mom had just come home from her second round in rehab. She was doing well but had lost her job as a nurse, and she'd have to look for work. I was feeling down, a bit depressed really, and was worrying about our upcoming senior year.

"Always," Brit said. She turned her attention back to her ice cream, licking around the sides of the cone. It was melting quickly in the heat.

"What if we end up going to different colleges that are far apart?" I said. "I don't have the money to go anyplace fancy, not now that Mom is out of work. You could be in New York, and I could be in…." I was about to say California, the farthest place away from her I could think of, when I realized I probably couldn't afford out-of-state tuition. "Here," I said. "I could still be *here*."

Brittney laughed. "No, you won't! You're brilliant, and any college would be crazy not to take you."

Her words made me feel better, but only a little.

"What if we do drift apart?" I said, suddenly serious. "People do that. You'll have your friends. I'll have mine. You might move out of state and have kids with Aaron—"

"Wait!" Brit said. "We are NOT engaged!"

"Not yet!" I said, and we laughed. Aaron was a nice guy, but I was just kidding about marriage. Who thinks of that in high school?

"But seriously, Brit. Things happen. People drift apart."

I tried then to imagine life without Brit. Since preschool, we had been inseparable. There were times in grade school when we weren't in the same class, and it was awful. But we still saw each other at lunch, during recess, and of course, after school. We were in Brownies together, then Girl Scouts in middle school. We took swimming lessons together when we were six and horseback riding lessons when we were eight. We've been part of each other's birthday celebrations. I've even traveled with her and her family to visit her grandmother in Tennessee during spring break.

"Hey," Brit said.

I licked my ice cream again, catching the drips before they reached my hand. Then I looked over at her. Her deep, brown eyes met mine.

"*Never.* I will never leave you, Heather. No matter how crazy your life gets, you can always count on me to be that one constant. I will always, *always* be here for you."

And for emphasis, she held up her left hand, which had that small white scar on her palm. I held up mine, with a bigger, matching scar.

The sun was setting, and its golden rays were shining on her hair at that moment, giving her the look of an angel. I felt a huge swell of love in my heart for this beautiful person, my sister, my best friend.

"Thank you," I said. And we went back to eating our ice cream and talking about boys, and school, and all the normal things teenage girls are supposed to talk about.

— — —

As I lie there in bed, trying to stay warm, I wonder where Brit is now.

Chapter 36

A darkness has settled over me. I'm starting to wonder if maybe my mom's depression is hereditary. For all of the months before this, I've always held out hope, but today I feel like giving up. Giving in.

I don't even have the energy to think about suicide.

When Tommy wakes us, I get dressed and eat the stale donuts provided. I say nothing on the car ride over to the motel, where I'll spend the next ten to fifteen hours providing an outlet for someone else's problems and addictions, and providing an income for Tommy. And us. The girls.

I'm providing for Chloe and Serena, and even Reg.

"Heather? Do you want a tattoo this weekend?" Tommy asks from the front seat. I wonder if he's referring to the tattoo like Chloe has. The one that marks me as his property. I shrug. Why not? What does it matter.

Tommy can sense a change in me, maybe, because he keeps talking. "How about we get your nails done, too? I know this place, where I take Chloe. You want to go?"

I shrug again. This is the first time he has offered to take me out. The other three girls get special treats from him every now and then, but for me, this is a first.

"Oh, let's!" Chloe says cheerfully.

"You can come, too," Tommy says to her. "Maybe I'll take all four of you. My treat. And we'll get your hair done. You want to add some color, Heather?"

It's important for us to look nice. That's what Chloe has told me. The clients don't want ugly girls.

I turn towards the window, not answering. I don't care about any of that. It's a sunny day today, but cold. February in

New York is brutal. The dress I have is sleeveless and the thin coat Tommy found for me doesn't provide much protection.

As the images speed by—boarded up buildings, people huddled against their walls, a bar, the pharmacy where I bought the pads—I don't notice any of it. I have gone inside myself today, and it feels nice in here. If I go in deep enough, I don't even feel the cold. I can't tell that my knees are shaking, and my teeth are chattering.

Tommy parks the car and opens the back door for me. As we run from the parking lot towards the motel room, I'm almost relieved to get there, to feel the blast of heat inside. He closes the door and leaves me alone to work. I keep my coat on, trying to warm up. I rub my arms with my hands, then take off my shoes and try to warm my feet the same way. It doesn't do much good, and I don't have much time. The first man will be here soon.

So I take my coat off and put my kitten heels back on. Then I sit on the bed and try to look provocative, like Reg showed me. Maybe I'll get a tip. Chloe told me that sometimes, if they're really happy with you, they leave a tip. I could use some extra money.

Then, as I hear a short knock on the door, and see the handle turning, I retreat back inside myself, to my safe place. And I don't come out again until I'm back in my bed at the house. It's a system that works. It's a system that I'm sticking with.

— — —

But Chloe doesn't come into my room that night. It's the first night she hasn't visited since I got there, with the exception of those nights she was too hurt to get out of bed. And then *I* visited *her.*

I wait for a while. Reg comes in and is soon asleep. I hear the men settle down and the muffled sound of Tommy's television playing in his room. One of the thugs leaves because I hear the front door close. After what seems like hours and Tommy's television has gone quiet, I get up and tiptoe down the hall to Chloe's room. Serena is in there, sleeping. Thug woke her early this morning to work, so I don't wake her.

Chloe hasn't come home.

I'm worried, but not overly. Sometimes Reg stays out longer than the rest of us. That's probably the case with Chloe. So she's probably okay. I go back to bed and lay there some more, trying to think about where Chloe could be. Eventually, sleep overtakes me.

— — —

"Where's Chloe?" I say the next morning. We're all sitting in the living room, sharing some breakfast bars that Thug Two brought in. What I wouldn't give for some fresh fruit! Reg is smoking her joint while eating, a trick she seems to have mastered. Serena is looking at the floor and is quiet, like always.

Tommy answers me. "She didn't come in last night." He has been pacing and keeps checking his phone.

"What do you mean?" I ask.

"Thug went to pick her up from the hotel, and she wasn't there. The room was empty. And she didn't come home last night. I drove around this morning but haven't seen her."

"Chloe's *missing?*" I say.

Tommy shrugs. "She'll turn up. This has happened a few other times. She goes home with one of the clients, or sometimes one of the other girls. Gets me some dirt."

Dirt is Tommy's name for heroin.

"She'll be fine," he says again.

But he looks worried. And I'm scared.

I have no choice but to go in to work, because Thug One is driving us to the hotel today, and he's in a mood. I feel sick inside at what might have happened to Chloe. I look down all the streets we pass and against the boarded-up buildings, hoping to see her small frame. When we get to the hotel, I scan the parking lot for clues. But nothing.

The shift seems harder than usual, and my skin crawls worse with each new man who enters my hotel room. I want to leave, to run and find Chloe, but Thug is standing guard, out in the parking lot, in his car. I wonder what he does in there for so many hours. I doubt he reads.

And if he leaves, there's always someone else. Always. There's no chance of escape.

Ever.

Which makes me wonder why no one saw Chloe. But maybe Chloe doesn't need a guard like I do. Maybe she stays put.

Tommy picks me up from the hotel around 2:30 a.m.

"Did you find her?" I ask as soon as I get in the car.

"No," he says, and lights up a cigarette. He reaches back and offers me a drag. I refuse.

I scan the streets as we drive, looking, hoping. I see a lot of girls working the street corners, but I don't see Chloe anywhere.

When Tommy stops the car, I refuse to get out. He's standing there, holding the door open, waiting.

"I want to go looking for her," I say. "We have to find her."

"No," he says simply, and motions for me to get out.

"Please."

Tommy reaches inside and grabs my wrist. He pulls me out. "That's *my* job," he says. "I take care of my girls, right?"

I'm not so sure he does, but I don't tell him this. I let him lead me inside, and I head to the bathroom. I take a quick shower. There isn't much shampoo left, and I have to add water to the bottle to get any out. My hair feels only partially clean because of this. But I don't care. My mind is on Chloe.

I turn the water off and am drying off when I hear shouting. Tommy and Thug One are yelling at each other.

"If something has happened to her, Sal, you owe me," Tommy shouts. "You never should have left the lookout. I'm holding you responsible for this." And then I hear a door slam.

When I open the bathroom door, I see Thug One sitting in one of the living room chairs with a beer in his hand and a cigarette in the other. Tommy is the one who left. Thug Two is standing, fishing through his pockets for keys.

"I'll check the alleyways and garbage bins," he says.

He leaves. His words sink in. Alleyways and garbage bins. Do they think she's dead? Do they think somebody dumped her body?

"What you looking at?" Thug One growls at me, and I realize I'm standing in the hall just inside the living room doorway. Just staring. Lost in my thoughts.

"Any word on Chloe?" I ask.

"Nope. Boss went to look for her again."

"Do you think…she's okay?"

Thug One takes a drink of beer before responding, then he doesn't even answer my question.

"Go to bed," he says.

I creep into my bedroom. Reg is out late tonight, so I'm alone with no one to talk to. The night is hot, and the window air conditioner in the living room isn't reaching the bedroom. I lie on top of the covers and will myself to fall asleep.

Chapter 37

I don't sleep all night, and when I get up, Reg doesn't look like she slept, either. She has dark circles under her eyes. But she's her usual stiff self and only shrugs when I try to talk to her.

In the car, I miss Chloe sitting in the spot between me and Reg. Neither of us speak. Reg stares out her window, and I look out mine. Tommy drops Reg off a few rooms down. Then he parks the car farther up and turns the ignition off so he can come and get me out.

But his cell phone rings.

He answers it. I hear a male voice on the other end, but I can't tell what the voice is saying.

"You sure?" Tommy says.

There's an answer on the other end. Tommy pounds the steering wheel and swears a violent string of words. I'm in the back seat, but I still cringe deep into the seat, away from his angry voice.

"Bring her to me," he says. "You know where I am."

Then he clicks his phone off and gets out of the car.

"Was that about Chloe?" I ask as he opens my door, and I stand.

He nods. I look into his eyes. His face is red, his eyes set to a steely brown. "She's dead."

"*What?*" I don't think I've heard him right.

"Dead. She got chopped. Somebody dumped her, and Franco found her body in a garbage bin."

"No," I feel my knees starting to buckle, but suddenly Tommy has me. He holds me up and pulls me towards the motel room.

"I need you to get in here before you pass out," he says. He beeps his keys, locking his car, then half pulls, half carries me to the motel room.

"Not Chloe," I say. The horror of what has just happened is sinking in. Chloe isn't coming back. Someone has hurt her. *Killed* her. And I have lost my only friend.

Her pale, round face comes into my mind. So young and so sweet. So confused. I think of her offering me food. Painkillers. Drugs. Anything to take care of me. And encouragement. Even if her help was misguided, her heart was in the right place.

Who will sit with me at night while I fall asleep? Who can I confide in?

"No," I say, sitting on the motel bed. I feel tears spill down my cheeks.

"I'll see you in ten hours," he says.

"Tommy, don't go," I say. I'm crying for real now. "I need to see her. I need to see her body. I have to be sure."

Tommy frowns, and for a moment he waivers. Then he shakes his head. "No. You need to work, especially now that I'm down a girl. And clean yourself up. You're a mess." He reaches over to the nightstand and throws a box of tissue at me. Then he shuts the door.

I blow my nose.

The doorknob turns, and I think that Tommy has changed his mind and come back. But it's not him. It's a dark-haired man in a business suit, with a subtle shadow of beard on his face.

"I can't," I say, as he closes the door behind him. He tosses a wad of cash on the bed. "My friend just died." I am crying harder now. Surely, he'll have some compassion on me. I wait for him to say something, to pat me on the shoulder maybe. But he takes his suit coat off and throws it across the chair near the door. Then he starts unbuckling his pants.

"Yes, you can," he says. "And you will. I'll get what I paid for, one way or another."

And he does. I give in to him because it hurts less that way. And as soon as he's done, as soon as he's leaving, I pull my dress down over my legs and jump off the bed. I run to the door and look out. There's Thug Two with his car parked next to Tommy's. They're looking in his trunk.

Surely they wouldn't really be looking at a dead body in the parking lot, would they? Or maybe they would, because nobody in this part of the city cares. Death is rampant here. Violence is the norm.

I push the John out of my way and run towards them, the gravel and cold blacktop cutting into my bare feet.

I'm crying as I reach the car, and there she is. Chloe. Her body, crumpled into the trunk. She's wearing a white dress with pearls sewn across the neckline, one she looked so pretty in and much older. And it's stained with blood. *Chloe's* blood. Around her neck is a huge bruise where someone choked her. And there's a stab wound in her side where her dress is torn. That must be where all the blood is from.

Tommy tries to push me away, but I see it before he can. I see the horrible marking running down the length of her left arm, just below the tattoo of Tommy's name. Someone has cut a word into the flesh of her arm. A message for Tommy. It reads: REVENGE.

— — —

I don't remember much more of the day. Tommy tells Thug Two to "take care of me" as he slams the trunk lid. "Then take care of *her*," he says, nodding to the body in the trunk. I can't think of it as Chloe anymore.

I fight Thug Two, screaming and trying to beat him with my fists. He's much stronger than I am, and twice my size, and he picks me up and carries me to the motel room. The door is already open, so he carries me through and throws me on the bed, kicking the door closed behind us.

"Pull yourself together!" he yells. But I can't. I can't stop crying, and I'm hysterical. I am wailing and trying to stand, but he keeps pushing me down. He'll probably beat me. He'll probably kill me, but I no longer care, because my only friend in this world of hell is dead, and now I'm utterly alone.

Thug Two jumps on the bed and pulls my arms down against my sides. Then he pins me down by putting his knees across my midsection, blocking my arms as well.. The pressure is cutting off my breath. With his hands he reaches in and pulls something out of his coat pocket. It's a rubber tube.

He's going to strangle me.

I fight harder, but he's too strong for me. Then instead of wrapping the tubing around my neck, he wraps it around my arm. The vein in my arm bulges. It's the one in the crook of my arm, on the other side of the elbow. They one they use to take blood when you go to the doctor's.

Then he pulls out a syringe and vial and fills the syringe. I suddenly realize what he's going to do. He's going to inject me with heroin. It'll look like I died of an overdose.

"No!" I scream. "I'll be good. I promise. I promise!" I'm begging him now. I don't want that drug. I don't want any drug. And suddenly I don't want to die.

But I can't stop him. He plunges the needle into my vein and pushes the fluid into me.

It doesn't take too long before it works. I feel a rush in my body, of warmth and sleepiness. But not death. Not yet. Suddenly the fight goes out of me, and I wonder why I'm even trying. By the time Thug Two releases me and leaves, I'm floating in a world of high, and I don't even care or count how many men I see.

Chapter 38

Dennis came to high school during our sophomore year. He was instantly targeted as a nerd, dressed in button-up striped shirts and glasses that he always pushed up on his nose with his index finger. He didn't make too many waves, and I didn't really notice him. I was busy getting good grades and hoping my mom didn't get swallowed up by her depression.

But I guess Dennis thought it would be fun to try out for a sport, and he picked basketball. It made sense, in a way, because he's tall. Almost six-feet. But he's super skinny and not really that athletic.

He tried, though, I'll give it to him. Brit had her eye on Aaron then, so we kept track of practices, sometimes sitting in the gym to watch practices from the bleachers. I did homework, my nose always in a book, and Brit did, too, but she also watched Aaron.

"Do you think he'll ever ask me out?" she said.

She and Aaron had a "thing" going for the past several months. He flirted with her in the hallways between classes, and she smiled her charming smile. But it was always a game, a dance, and so far nothing had come of it. Some of our friends said that Aaron was shy, which it turned out he is. Not super shy, but shy around girls. And Brit is drop-dead gorgeous, so I can see why he would be afraid of rejection.

Although if he had any sense he could see that she liked him by the way she acted.

But we watched Dennis at practices, and he was always dropping ball, or if he got it up to the basket, his shot didn't go in. The guys cut him some slack, but you could tell he wasn't really "one of them."

"Brainiac has slippery fingers today," Mark Cosak said one afternoon, so loud that we heard it in the bleachers.

"Just today?" one of the others said, and most of the other guys laughed. Brit and I glanced at each other, and I could read her mind: *Immature idiots,* she was thinking.

I nodded in agreement and went back to my work.

Aaron never made fun of him, which is another reason Brit liked him. We decided Aaron must have some class.

And he did. Because for Sweetest Day that year, Aaron bought Brit a dozen roses and a ticket to go with him to the homecoming dance. He was waiting with both for her in the parking lot one morning when I drove her to school. He was standing near the front entrance to the school, looking nervous. When he saw us, he turned a few shades of pale.

"What's he up to?" Brit asked. I could tell she was one part worried and one part excited. Were the flowers for her?

Turns out they were. The two went to the dance together and have been together since.

Later that winter, basketball tryouts came, and of course Dennis didn't make it. He went back off my radar for a while. Until that dreaded day in class when he told the players' passwords to everybody.

I remember the talk in the hallway. "I'm gonna kill him." "Nerd boy has gotten himself in too deep." "I'll use his face for a goal post." "Idiot."

So they waited in the gym to give him a swirly. And to his good luck, Aaron was there to save him. Because he was the co-captain of the basketball team, he had earned some respect, and the other guys let Dennis go, although regretfully.

The next day Dennis wandered over to our table.

"Hey," he said casually to Aaron.

Aaron looked up. "Hey."

"I um…hey, thanks for yesterday."

I glanced up. A lot of people were staring at us. The entire table of football guys, some of them with their necks cranked around to see. The cheerleaders were looking our way and giggling. Aaron's team members… most of them had stopped eating or talking to see what Aaron would do.

182

"No big deal," Aaron said, and took a bite of his sandwich. I saw his eyes dart around, catching what was going on. But Aaron wasn't one to care what others thought. He was popular enough, strong enough, and confident enough that he could pretty much do what he wanted to do. So he made a big choice that day

"Have a seat," he said, gesturing with his sandwich towards the seat across from him.

Dennis glanced around nervously. "Are you sure?" he said quietly.

"Sit," Aaron said firmly.

Dennis did. And that's when we found out what a nice guy he really is.

— — —

Tommy won't say what he did with Chloe's body, but Reg has ideas.

The three of us girls are huddled in Serena's room, sitting on her bed. None of us can sleep. Not after what happened to Chloe. It's about 4 a.m., and the men are all quiet. Tommy went in his bedroom and shut the door when we got home around 3 a.m. We haven't heard from him since. I have no idea where the thugs are, but the last time I looked, one of them was on the couch snoring. Probably still is.

So Reg and I decided to sneak into Serena's room to talk. The heroin Thug Two gave me wore off long ago, and I'm left with a pounding headache, which could be from all the stress.

Reg is smoking something new. She hasn't cried yet, but she has new, hard lines around her eyes that I haven't seen before. "He burned the body," Reg says confidently.

The thought horrifies me.

"How do you know?" I ask.

"That's what he did with the last girl."

"What last girl?" I ask. I've been crying for hours. Not hard tears, but small ones keep sneaking out and running down my face. I can't seem to stop. My nose is all snotty, and my ears are plugged from all the blowing. I've used up a lot of our toilet paper because we don't have tissues. Oddly,

Serena is quiet, wrapped tightly in her blanket and rocking a little bit. I'm worried about her.

"The one that was here before you came."

I hadn't thought of someone being here before me. Was I a replacement?

"Why would he burn the body?" I hear my voice shaking when I speak. "How? Where?" These are questions that I don't really want to know the answers to, and yet somehow I need to. I need to know that Chloe's body isn't somewhere rotting in a garbage dump.

Reg shrugs, and I'm once again frustrated at her lack of communication. I can see her in the dim light from her joint, and also from the weak light around the window shade. The moon is out tonight. It's an unseasonably warm evening.

"Serena? Are you okay?" I ask for the fourth time in the past twenty minutes.

She nods but continues rocking.

"Here," Reg says. She offers Serena her joint. After a moment, Serena reaches out for it and inhales. She holds the smoke inside her for a while, then slowly exhales. Then she does it again. When she's finished, she hands it to me.

I glance at Reg, and she nods. My head is pounding, and my heart is breaking. I think of the merciless men who refused to let me grieve today. I think of Tommy pushing me away and slamming the trunk on the body of my one and only friend in this dark place. And I think of my mom and friends back home. Chloe is right. No one is looking for me. I've been here a year, and no one has come for me. They've given up. They probably think I'm dead.

This is now my life.

So I take the joint and inhale. Almost immediately I feel the drugs lifting me up. Reg usually laces her joints with heroin. None of us ask where she gets it. She just always seems to have some.

Within seconds I feel better. The pain goes away, in both my head and my heart. I take another drag, holding it in my lungs for a while, like Serena did. Then I exhale, and hand it back to Reg. She smiles a little bit.

"Feel better?" she asks.
"Yes." I do.
As a matter of fact I feel a lot better.

Chapter 39

Something in me breaks the night Chloe dies.

Tommy wakes me up the next morning for work, and I'm hit with the memory that Chloe is gone. The image of the word "revenge" dug into her arm haunts me, and no matter how tightly I close my eyes I can still see her lifeless eyes and the blood on her white dress.

I get up and immediately dig into my underwear pile, where I've stashed the drugs I save to sell. I sort through them. Coke. Weed. Here it is. A small bit of heroin.

Reg is sitting up, rubbing the sleep out of her eyes.

"How do I do this?" I ask her. "How do I make it into a joint?"

She opens her nightstand drawer and pulls out a few tampons. Inside of one, she has stuffed some rolling papers. Inside the other one is some heroin of her own and some weed. Clever.

She hands me a paper. Then she slowly makes one up out of her drugs. I sit on my bed and watch carefully, imitating what she does. Soon I have my first hand-made smoke. My joint isn't as neatly rolled as hers is, but it's not bad.

I get ready and go out into the living room, rolling the joint in between my fingers. If Tommy notices, he doesn't care. He lets us have drugs, *encourages* it even, but I have never made my own and for a moment I'm afraid he's going to ask where I *got* the drugs. If he knew I have been stashing what he gives me so I could sell instead of using them, he'd kill me.

So I light it, and practice smoking in between eating my donut.

Somehow, with the drugs in me, it doesn't seem so tragic that Chloe is gone. The hurt is still there, the grief, but it's buried somewhere deep inside me. It's like I'm standing on the outside looking at it. It's weird, but it works.

———

Three days later a new girl shows up. She's blond and skinny and terrified. She's wearing nice clothes, so I don't think this one came from off the streets. Tommy introduces her to us at noon, just as we're about to leave.

"This is a mistake," she says. "I…I want to go home."

I wonder if it was Cory who lured her in.

Tommy walks into the kitchen for a moment. Kaitlyn glances at the front door, but both the thugs are guarding it, standing there with arms crossed looking like tough dudes.

"That man—Tommy—he says if I do a job for him it'll be okay," she whispers to us. "That I have to do what he asks, and then things will go smoother for me. What…what do you think the job is?"

Her voice is shaking. I glance down at her carefully manicured fingernails and see that her hands are shaking as well. Her skin is clear, her hair is clean. She's not from around here. She's from somewhere else. A family is missing her right now, I'll bet.

I think about Chloe, and how she helped me get settled in here. She showed me the ropes and helped me out.

"Here." Instead of answering Kaitlyn, I reach my arm out and offer her my joint. "This will make it easier."

She shakes her head. "I don't do drugs."

"Not yet," Reg says.

"Take it," I say, but I'm pulling my arm back a little bit. It's the only one I have. I'm not sure I want to share it.

She shakes her head again, and then Tommy's back. He takes her by the wrist and pulls her out the door. "Trust me," he says to her as the door closes, but I hear her start screaming for help. Thug One grins, and I want to punch him. Thug Two goes outside, probably to assist Tommy.

187

The car door slams. And I know where Tommy is taking her. He's taking her to her first day of hell.

— — —

Kaitlyn sleeps in Serena's room, in Chloe's bed. She came home last night and curled up in a ball and cried all night. I wanted to go to her, but I was too high. And too tired. It seems all I want to do is sleep.

— — —

Three days after Kaitlyn arrives, almost a week after Chloe died, I run out of drugs.

"Can I borrow some?" I ask.

"No," Reg says.

"I'll pay you back." I'm feeling agitated and nauseas. And I'm trembling.

"No," she says again.

So when Reg goes into the bathroom to get ready, I open her nightstand drawer and look for the tampons. They're there, but there's nothing inside them. She has moved her stash.

I'm feeling desperate now. Tommy has taken Kaitlyn out, but soon one of the thugs will come to get us, and I can't go to that hotel without my high. I can't. I won't survive another day.

Panicked, I creep into the kitchen.

"Heather, we have to go!" Thug One shouts as I pass by him in the living room.

"I just need a drink of water," I say back. Then I glance over my shoulder. No one can see me, so I quickly open the cupboard under the sink. There they are—the coffee cans. My heart is pounding rapidly in my chest as I pop the lid off. I take a $100 bill out and cram it into my bra before putting the lid back on. The I close the cupboard door and stand. I run some water for added benefit and clank a glass.

Then I go out into the living room. Reg is there, waiting for me. Serena and Kaitlyn are gone.

"Let's go," Thug One says, and we follow him out to the car.

"I need to stop at the store," I say.

"For what?"

"Tampons."

The men don't like to discuss "female issues," as they call them, so he grunts, but he does stop on the way to the motel. This is the one that Chloe told me about. The one where I bought my feminine napkins and the ibuprofen that didn't work. But she also told me it's a good place to pick up some Smack.

I walk in. The balding clerk is stacking cigarettes onto a shelf behind the counter. I approach him.

"I'm here for some Smack," I say quietly.

He raises an eyebrow. "I have no idea what you're talking about. The candy bars are over there," and he nods in the direction.

I lay the $100 bill down flat on the counter, my hand covering it.

He looks at it, chewing on his cigarette. Then he disappears into the back room and returns with a small box. He slides it to me.

"I'll need some papers to roll it with," I say. "And I'd like a baggie of those little white pills too."

He disappears again and brings back two small baggies. One has papers and the other has pills. I palm the small box and slip the baggies into my bra. He takes the $100 bill. I have no idea if he owes me change, but when he doesn't offer, I turn to leave.

"Wait a minute," I say. Then I go and pick up a box of sanitary pads and add a box of condoms to make it look good if Thug checks what I was doing in here.

"I need these too."

"Pay up," he says. He holds out his hand.

I don't have any more money.

"I gave you enough," I say firmly, hoping that's the truth.

Our eyes lock for a moment. Then I say, "I'll be back for more. I can pay you then."

After about five seconds a grin spreads across his face, like it took him a moment to realize what I just said. He nods. I leave.

"What took so long?" Thug One says.

"Nothing. I had trouble finding them. Then I had to go in the bathroom and put one in."

"Okay, enough!" he says, cringing at my words, like hearing about a menstruating woman is the grossest thing in his life.

Reg raises one eyebrow in question, but I ignore her. I wonder if she knows the real reason I went in there.

Chapter 40

There has been no time all night for me to roll my joint. I've had to survive on the little white pills, which are fine "I don't care" pills, but they don't last long. And there's another John on the way.

So I sit on the edge of the motel bed and swallow the pill that will help me relax. My shaking hand sloshes the water in the glass.

I am scared all the time.

Fear is constantly clawing at my stomach. Sometimes it's quiet. Sometimes it shouts at me. The pills help quiet its voice. But it seems like since Chloe died, it's harder to quiet. That's why I'm craving the heroin.

There's a single knock on the door, and it opens. A man walks in, and my stomach flip-flops. He is here early, and the pill hasn't had time to take effect yet. The last one wore off already.

I've never seen this man before. Sometimes I get repeats, but he's new. He's dressed in wrinkled khaki pants and a button down. He looks cleaner than most, but not by much. His dark eyes drink me in, and he smiles.

"You're Heather?"

I don't answer him. Instead, I lay back on the bed and hope it's over quickly.

— — —

The man doesn't stay long. I sit up, waiting for the room to steady before I stand. I'm still sitting there five minutes later when Tommy walks into the room. He opens the door so ordinary girl

hard it bangs against the wall. I'm relieved to see it's him and not a random stranger.

But he doesn't look happy. I get a twisty feeling in my stomach.

He stalks over to the bed, and through the haze of drugs I'm starting to notice that he's angry with me. He *knows*. He knows I took the money.

"Slut!" he grabs my hair and yanks me into a sitting position. The sudden jerk hurts my neck. "Thief!" He slaps me sharply across the face, and my eyes start to water. Part of my brain feels the pain. The other part of it is wandering around in the fog.

"I needed to buy condoms…" I begin, but he yanks on my hair. I put the condoms on the dresser when I first got here. They sit there as proof of my story. To cover the lie.

"You only *need* what I give you, do you understand?" He sits down so he is right next to me. I feel his breath on my face. It stinks of garlic.

We're not supposed to buy anything for ourselves. Ever.

My eyes water more. That twisty feeling in my stomach is still there. I think I might throw up.

"Do you *understand?*" He shouts it into my face, his spittle wetting my cheek. I nod.

"Good." He lets go of my hair, and I fall limply back onto the bed. "You have to work it off." He gets up off the bed and finds my dress, crumpled on the floor. He throws it at me. "Get dressed. I'll drop you off."

I know what that means. Chloe told me once. If you don't make your quota for the day, he sends you out on the streets.

I remember the two men who picked her up. Who nearly beat her to death. I don't want to go out on the streets.

I sit up and reach for the dress, but he sits back down on the bed. He raises his hand, and I flinch, but then he tenderly strokes my cheek. "I know what's best for you, right?" he says in a soft, overly sweet voice.

I nod, because he does. Because he will beat me if I say he doesn't. The strap of my slip has fallen off of my shoulder. My right breast is exposed. Tommy puts his hand on the back of my neck and pulls me towards him, kissing me hard on

192

the mouth. I taste blood from where he slapped me. Then he pushes me down and is on top of me. His weight is crushing me. I can feel his hands exploring, but I'm not really sure where. Part of me wants to fight through the drug's haze, to get up, to run. But the other side of my brain tells me to stay put. It's safer that way.

"You love, me, right?" he whispers into my ear. The stubble on his face is rough. His hand reaches down and unzips his jeans.

I can't speak to answer him. His weight is too much. But I know that *he* loves *me*. He is here, touching me. Proving it. He gives me things. Money. Food. And drugs to make it all better. He will keep me safe.

He'll hurt me He'll help me He'll hurt me

He pulls up my slip, and I close my eyes, letting my mind take me somewhere else, giving into the pull of the drugs. They take me away, and I'm no longer aware of the man who is ripping out my soul.

— — —

When he is finished, we lay there in bed together, smoking. The joint he brought with him has something extra in it, and I'm glad for it. This way I won't have to smoke mine.

I can feel it lifting me higher than usual. There's a slight tingling sensation in my head. I'm trying to explore this feeling when he rolls over and sits up, taking the joint with him. He extinguishes it on the wooden headboard behind us. I smell burning plastics, and now there's an ugly black spot in the fake wood.

Tommy grabs the crumpled one-hundred-dollar bill that is still laying on the dresser, knocking over the box of condoms in the process. Then he walks over to the chair and opens my purse, pulling out the money I made today. $1500. He stuffs it in his jacket pocket and zips it up.

"Get dressed and get in the car," he says. He leaves, shutting the door behind him. I find my underwear lying on the floor and put them on. Then I quickly pull on my dress.

I'm a little wobbly from the drugs, and I almost fall over. But that's okay. They make it okay.

I leave and go out to the parking lot. It's dark outside. Tommy is quiet when I get in the car, and he doesn't look at me. He starts driving.

"I want to go home," I say, meaning the dirty house on Side Street that we live in. I don't want to beg. But I do. Because I know what's coming. "*Please*. I'll pay you back for the money I took. I'll find a way."

"You know the rules," he says.

Not the street. Not tonight. Fear clenches my stomach again, fighting for dominance over the drugs.

He drives me to the corner of Burton and Straight. The shops are all boarded up. Across the street from us, a few people are leaning against the wall of what used to be a florist shop. They're smoking something. Tommy pulls up to the curb and stops the car. He looks at me. "Get to work."

This is the same corner we were on when Chloe was taken by those two creeps. What if they come back?

I numbly open the car door and climb out. It's early spring, and cold wind is biting through my dress. The kitten heels I'm wearing don't give me much warmth, and I know that soon my feet will be freezing. As I shut the door, I look at Tommy one last time, hoping.

Please.

But he speeds away, leaving me standing alone on the corner, waiting for the next John to come along and buy me more time.

Chapter 41

I watch the few cars in fear, wondering who's out at this time of morning. I'm looking for the creeps who picked up Chloe. Or the ones who killed her. How will I know who they are? Will I recognize their car before they get to me?

This dark hour of the morning you don't usually get the businessmen. You get the lowest of the low; the creatures of the dark. The men who call nighttime *their hour.*

But the next car that drives by is a cop car. A sharp zap of adrenaline shoots through me. "The cops aren't your friends," says a voice. "Jail is worse than here." That's Chloe speaking. "Don't let them find you."

I turn to run, but my legs are wobbly, and I trip, falling and skinning my knee.

"Hey," says a male voice. I glance back. It's one of the cops. He's getting out of his car. "Stop!"

I stand and start running down the sidewalk, past the boarded-up buildings and heading for an alleyway up ahead. I hear him coming after me, his shoes pounding on the pavement.

"Stop!" he shouts again.

I'm almost to the dark alleyway. I can turn in there and lose him. But what—or who —is waiting for me *there?* I hesitate as a vision of the balding cop comes back at me.

"Cops are your friends," says Mrs. Kettle.

But I have drugs on me. They're in my bra. Heroin. Possession equals prison time. How many times has Tommy pounded that into our heads?

I put on a burst of speed and feel my lungs burning. I'm making good time, but then my heel gets caught in a crack in the pavement. It snaps off, and I pitch forward. I throw my hands out to break my fall, and my palms hit the pavement just milliseconds before my knees do. The rough pavement takes the skin off both palms and both knees, and I realize I've ripped my stockings.

Tommy will be mad.

The police officer is bending over, grabbing me by the wrist and pulling me up. The pill I took, along with the joint Tommy shared with me, is making me really woozy. The world is spinning.

And I think I forgot to eat today.

"What's this?" the police officer says, and I see my drugs have fallen out of my bra and are laying on the sidewalk. He pulls on my wrist. "Whoring for drugs, huh?"

Just as I stand, the world tips sideways and fades to black.

Chapter 42

When I wake up, I'm back in the ER, the same one I was in when I overdosed. I carefully wiggle my fingers, then my toes. Everything seems to be working. I don't feel as bad as I did then.

I carefully turn my head sideways, but nothing spins. I see Tommy leaning against the wall out in the hallway. He's waiting for me. He'll take me home.

I look for the police, but they're gone. Then I start to itch my nose and realize my left hand is handcuffed to the side of the bed.

"You're awake," says a nurse. She's petite and blond but has a tired, lined face. "You got yourself a little too high. They're going to let you sober up a bit before they take you in,"

"Take me in?" My throat is dry and scratchy. I try to swallow. I need some water.

"Yep," the nurse says. "You've got yourself in a mess. Possession. Honey, you girls gotta stop selling yourselves for drugs. Now you're looking to do time."

I frantically glance at Tommy. The nurse follows my eyes.

"Him? He's probably gonna try to bail you out. You're making too much money for him to let you go. But I doubt it'll work. This your first rap? Second?"

I have no idea what she's talking about. But then she hands me a cup of water and raises my bed a little bit so I can sip from the straw.

"I'm going to give you this to help you detox," she says, and fills a syringe. Before I can protest, she plunges it in my arm.

I glance again at Tommy, and our eyes meet. He looks tired to me. For the first time ever, I see him as a person. Someone else who probably didn't end up where he thought he would. I mean, what little boy wants to grow up selling women for a living? Wanting to live in a world of lies and drugs and sex? I think of the ugly word "revenge" carved into Chloe's small arm. And I think of all of the people who hate Tommy.

Including me.

And yet I know that when they release me from here, if I'm not in jail, I'll go back home with him tonight.

I close my eyes and bid sleep to come.

— — —

In my dream I'm fourteen years old, and Brittney and I are at our first concert. It's a dream I have over and over because it was one of my favorite days ever.

Brit's dad took us to see Imagine Dragons. I have no idea where he got the tickets, because online they were super expensive, but he did, and there we were. We were in the nosebleed seats, but it was *so cool*, and we felt very teenager-ish, if that's even a word.

He bought us each a pop and a band t-shirt. The concert was great, and Brit and I sang along with several of the songs.

Then afterwards, even though it was 11:30 p.m. he went through a fast-food drive-thru on the way home and bought us burgers, fries and shakes. We listened to the Imagine Dragons CD in the car really loud and ate and talked about the concert. Brit's dad was so fun, and that night stands out in my memory as one of my favorite times ever.

In my dream tonight, we're at the fast-food drive-thru, and it's here when I usually wake up. But tonight in my dream, the car stalls.

"What are you girls doing?" a voice says. Brit and I are sitting in the backseat, and I turn to the voice. There's a creepy man in a business suit with a shadow of a beard staring in my window. I try to roll it up, but I can't.

Suddenly I'm afraid. "Brit, we have to get out of here!" I say, and when I turn to look at her, she's dressed in Chloe's white dress, and there's blood on it.

Then I look in the front seat, and Tommy's driving the car. I try the door handle, but it's locked. I'm trapped in the back seat.

"Brit!" I scream. The creepy man is reaching through the window to grab me. "Brit, help! They're going to hurt us!"

"We're fine," Brit says, and she's smoking a joint.

"No, we're not!" My heart is pounding as I'm trying to make Brittney understand how much danger we're in. I won't let Tommy have her, too. Not Brit.

"Stop!" I say, and I start pounding Tommy on the back of the head with my hands. But in my dream, it doesn't seem to have any effect.

"Heather, what are you doing?" Brit says. Her voice is calm.

"I'm trying to save you!" I say.

"Honey, I'm here to save *you*. Didn't I promise I'd never leave you?" Brit says.

Then the car becomes big enough so she can stand up. "Let her go," Brit says to Tommy. She puts her hands on her hips in that bossy way she has, and I hear her voice say, "I want to see all the girls you have, and I won't take no for an answer!"

All the girls? I look in the backseat, and suddenly it's filled with girls. There's me and Reg and Serena and Kaitlyn. And a lot of other girls I don't know. The car has become so big that it's more like an auditorium now.

"I mean it, and if you don't comply, I will be back, and you won't like what you see then!" Brit says. Her voice seems unnaturally loud.

"Ma'am, we can't just let anybody back there..." a voice is saying. It sounds like my nurse.

I open my eyes and realize I'm awake now. Brit's voice is still ringing in my ears. It's almost like she was here. I miss her so much. I miss her and my mom and Aaron and Dennis. I miss my job at the cafe and Jess and Cherise. I wonder what they're all doing now? My friends will all be in college. No, it's February. Or March? So Brit will be over halfway through her second semester. Wow, her first year nearly in at Columbia. I wonder how she liked it.

I close my eyes and feel tears fall down the sides of my face. I don't even try to brush them away. I just want this to end. If I can't die here, now, then I want Tommy to come and get me, and I want to smoke my joint and curl up in my bed in the house. I want to pretend I don't exist anymore.

I want to disappear.

I fold my fingers into my left palm, and I can feel the edges of the scar that bonded me and Brit as sisters. "I will always be there for you," Brit had said in life, and in my dream. But where is she now?

"Heather?"

The voice is soft. Disbelieving. It sounds like it's right above me. I open my eyes and standing above me, looking down, is Brittney.

"Heather!" Suddenly tears start to flow from her eyes, and she's laughing and crying at the same time. "Heather! I found you!"

I squint up at her. She looks different. Her hair is shorter, and she's straightened it. It hangs just above her shoulders. And she looks older. There's a crease running between her eyes that wasn't there before.

"Heather, it's me!"

I can't believe it. I wonder if I'm hallucinating from the drugs. But then she takes my right hand in her left, and I see her scar. The light crescent moon on her own palm. Her hand is warm, and she squeezes mine.

"Brittney?" I say. I'm still a little fuzzy.

"Yes!" She's crying now. She bends over the bed until her face is on my chest. She's hugging me the best she can and crying, and I suddenly realize that this is real. Brittney is real, and she's here. "I found you! I can't believe I finally found you!"

"You found me?"

"Yes, you silly girl! Didn't I promise never to forget you? To always be here for you?"

And here she is. I'm suddenly crying, and the nurse has now realized that we know each other. She asks Brit to raise up so she can prop my bed up. Then I'm sitting up, and there is Brit. I'm really awake, and she's really here.

"It's okay, now," Brit says, still crying. "You're safe. Heather, you're safe. We found you. Oh, I really should call your mom."

She has some papers in her other hand and lays them down on my bed so she can pull her phone out. One is a poster with my senior photo and "MISSING PERSON" printed across the top of it. The other is a brochure for Hope's Angels, an anti-human trafficking organization.

"My mom's okay?" I ask. I'm having trouble taking all of this in.

Brit looks at me as the phone is ringing. "Your mom is great! Wait until you see her." She grabs my hand again. "And you're safe now, Heather. It's over. I'm going to take you home."

I nod, the tears still running down my face. Then I glance out into the hall, but Tommy is gone.

Epilogue

ONE YEAR LATER

It's a warm Saturday in early June. It has been a little over two years since I was taken, and one since Brit found me. We're celebrating my twentieth birthday today in my backyard. I'm surrounded by friends. My mom looks amazing. She's two years clean and sober, and I haven't seen her this happy since before Daddy died.

The Hudsons are here, and Mrs. Hudson brought over all kinds of yummy food, like her homemade cheese ball and crackers, potato salad and sandwich rolls. Mom made me a chocolate cake from scratch instead of a box and put a lot of frosting on it. She decorated it with purple flowers and green icing leaves. It's the most beautiful thing ever.

Brit is here with Aaron, and Dennis came with a girl he met in college this past year. She's quite pretty and dotes on Dennis. It seems college has been good for him. He's studying computer science at MIT and couldn't be happier.

Aaron made it onto a college basketball team and has been playing for U of M. He's studying sports science and thinks he wants to be a physical therapist.

My mom hasn't used drugs since the day she found out I disappeared. Apparently Mrs. Hudson gave her a long talk about how she had to sober up if she ever wanted to find me. So Mom worked really hard those first few weeks, giving the police all the information she had to track me down, while detoxing. It was really difficult for her, Mrs. Hudson says, but she has worked hard and never looked back. After two years of being sober, she was reinstated as a nurse last month. She works in the new baby ward at the hospital and loves it.

During those first two months when I was gone, Brittney, Dennis and Aaron also worked really hard to find me. Aaron made a gazillion posters and hung them up everywhere. Then he posted tons of stuff online about me being lost. They even have a special website dedicated to finding me.

Dennis used his computer-oriented brain to figure out where my last phone signal really came from. He explained to the FBI what he had done to change my GPS location. They worked on it, and somehow they traced it to the state of New York. Brittney gave the police the description of Cory's car, and with the help of my café coworkers and a description of Cory himself, somehow, amazingly, the police found Cory three months after I disappeared. They could never have done it without Dennis, his information, and my friends.

Cory and his "dad" Roger (who wasn't really his dad) were arrested. They were part of a group of men who lured girls into trafficking situations. Mr. Sneeder, who I thought was my friend, was a plant in the coffee shop to find out information about me. Like what I told him about not getting into college, and what I want to study, and about my dad dying. He fed this information to Cory, who then came in and "coincidentally" had a lot in common with me. Mr. Sneeder knew the right time to call Cory in; when I was the most vulnerable. The day I was so down from all that was happening in my life, Cory came in to distract me. Once Cory built up my trust, and got me to go away with him, he took me to the house in New York. That was a brothel of sorts, where men paid big money to hook up with women, especially virgins. And after that, we girls were moved on, or sold, to people like Tommy.

I can't believe I was stupid enough to fall for that. But my therapist tells me that it happens all the time. And that I wasn't stupid. That it was a well laid out plan, a trap. Thousands of kids fall into trafficking every year in our country. Some of them are just ordinary girls like me.

Mom speaks, breaking me out of my thoughts.

"Are you ready, Heather?" she asks. I smile and nod. Everybody sings happy birthday to me, and I blow out my candles. Then Mom starts slicing through the cake.

"Which piece do you want?" she says, although she already knows.

"She wants the middle piece, of course," Brittney says. I look over at my friend, who is scooping ice cream.

Brittney is my hero. She deferred her first year of college, even though Columbia had given her a scholarship. The FBI found out I had been trafficked about the time she graduated from high school. Shortly after graduation, she hooked up with an organization called Hope's Angels, the one I saw on the brochure she brought with her to the hospital. It's a non-profit dedicated to finding victims of trafficking and helping them get out. They have a lot of volunteers now and even a board which Brit was recently elected to. Brit works at the coffee shop where I worked but has been taking her weekends and traveling around the big cities of Detroit, Houston, Miami, but mostly in New York, looking for me on street corners, in hospitals, and in motel rooms. There are photos of me up everywhere in these cities, I hear. Jess at the coffee shop has given Brit a flexible schedule so she can take off whenever she gets a tip. And a tip is what saved me.

Someone had seen my poster and reported me a few months before Brit found me. We don't know who. Perhaps a cop. Or one of the other girls. Or even a John. So she had been coming to that part of New York every chance she got for the past several months. The night she found me, a police officer had called the number on one of her posters. The partner of the cop who picked me up thought he recognized me, and when he called, Brit just happened to be in town. His call saved my life.

My friends didn't give up on me. Instead, they dedicated that year of their lives to finding me. I think of how grateful I am for all of them, and to be here, alive.

As I blow out my candles, I make a wish. It's a wish that all of the girls—and there are some boys, too—that all of them out there in this dark world can be found and come home. Safe. To friends and a mom like mine.

After Brit found me, she brought me home by ambulance, all the way to Detroit. I was malnourished and had very low iron. And I was strung out on drugs. They put me in rehab, and the first few weeks were hell, as I detoxed and tried to regain strength. After a poor diet for so long, the fresh fruit and vegetables they fed me weren't agreeing with me, and I felt sick most of the time. My body was too weak to heal. I had a nutritionist and drug counselor and a trauma counselor all working with me. It was a long hard six weeks, but then they finally let me come home and switch to outpatient therapy.

Gracie was so excited to see me she clung to me for days. She kept herself wrapped around my legs while I sat in the house, and she curled up beside me when I slept. She still won't let me out of her sight when I'm home.

I told the police here about Tommy and the girls, and they went back and looked around the neighborhood near the hospital where Brit found me but didn't see anything. So, after I got out of rehab, I made Brit take me back to that neighborhood. We took some police officers with us and drove around the area of the hospital until I saw something that looked familiar. It was the motel. From there I was able to find my way back to the house on Straight Street.

Tommy was gone, and so were the girls. The place was cleared out. We drove the streets, looking for them, and Brit and I went back several more times to drive around. I even stopped at the motel and asked. Nobody had seen Reg or Serena or Kaitlyn. At least nobody would admit to it.

We found Kaitlyn's family. She had been abducted one night while jogging along a park path in New Jersey. They have ramped up the search for her, and Brit's organization is helping. We will find her. We have to.

I'm different now. I still have nightmares every night and wake up terrified. I'm afraid Tommy will come through the door, or I imagine a man standing over my bed. I'm still in counseling, and they are doing some REM therapy which works with eye movements. It's supposed to be good for people who have gone through trauma.

I started working at a little veterinary office down on Main Street. I get to check in the cats and dogs and weigh them and stuff like that. It's quiet there, and I love it. It's only part time, since my therapist says I need to start slow. I'm going to enroll in the community college this fall and maybe take some science classes. I still might be a doctor. But I'm leaning more towards becoming a psychologist who works with victims of sexual abuse. I don't know yet.

I can't go back to the coffee shop where it all started, even though Brit works there. She says she stays there to be sure no creeps come in to steal girls again. But this fall, Brit is going to Columbia University. She's going to get her degree in law so she can actively work towards the causes she holds so dear. She wants to start by ending trafficking.

Sometimes at night, when I lay in bed awake, I think about Chloe and wish she could have lived just a little bit longer so I could have saved her. And because Brit believes that prayer led her to me, I have started praying. I pray for Reg, and Serena, and Kaitlyn. I'm even getting to the point where I can pray for Tommy. My counselor says that when I can finally let go of the hate, I will really start to heal.

"It's time to open presents!" Mom says. Jess, my former manager, is grinning. She grabs her present and puts it on the table in front of me. It's big. I don't know for sure, but I'm suspecting it's a cappuccino maker. Jess knows I love my coffee.

I look around at my loved ones: Mrs. and Mrs. Hudson and their son Timmy. Aaron, Dennis, Jess, Cherise, and of course, Brit. Brittney catches my eye and smiles.

And I am grateful. I have finally come home.

THE END

Acknowledgments

This book was difficult to write, not only because of the subject matter, but because I had to learn about a world of which, thankfully, I have no personal experience. I want to thank the people who taught me by sharing their *own* personal experiences. These women survivors who bravely told their stories to me not only filled in the blanks so I could write a factual novel, but their spirit and strength has inspired me. You are my heroines, and I am grateful that you are willing to step out of your comfort zone so that others can be free.

I also want to thank those who stepped inside Heather's world as readers:

Thank you to my first readers: Xanthe, Other Pam, and Sarah for reading the many early drafts until I found Heather's voice. Your insights helped me frame this story into something that makes sense. And thank you to my husband Duane, who read the very first draft and offered me a man's perspective.

To my beta readers: Anna, Emma, Rachel, Rochelle and Robyn. You gave me the perspective of a reader and helped me finish this story.

A special thank you to Anita Hoepner of Sparrow Freedom Project for her courage, honesty, insight, and compassion. When words fail, art speaks. And to Mike Ball of Lost Voices, for his continuing journey to help survivors heal through music.

I am forever grateful to my husband Duane and my two sons, Zack and Logan, for bringing joy and love into my life. And thank you to my parents, Floyd and Judy, who provided me with a safe, loving home to grow up in. I know how blessed I am, and I hope I never take this life for granted.

And thank you to God, for making each of us in His image and loving us unconditionally. Even when we're in our darkest moments, we are His, and we're never alone. There is always hope. *He heals the brokenhearted and binds up their wounds.* – Psalm 147:3

Resources

Victims of human trafficking are controlled by their traffickers through force or fear, and are often lured by false promises of money, stability, or a loving relationship. Girls and women aren't the only victims; so are men, boys, and transgender people. Also, trafficking isn't always for sex. Some traffickers want people for labor.

Identify Human Trafficking Victims

There are many different indicators that someone is a victim. Here are a few. If you suspect something is wrong, ask yourself these questions:

- Are there bruises or other signs of physical abuse?
- Is the person fearful, anxious, depressed, or showing other signs of psychological abuse?
- Is the person submissive?
- Is the person being controlled by someone?
- Does the person have very few personal possessions?
- Is the person being deprived of food, water, sleep, medical care, or other life necessities?
- Is the person allowed to be in public alone?
- Can the person freely contact friends or family?
- Is the person a minor engaged in commercial sex?
- Does a minor appear to be in a relationship with a much older person?
- Does the person fear his or her employer?
- Is there drug use?
- Can the person leave their job situation if they want?
- Has someone threatened the person's family?
- Do this person have an unusual tattoo that resembles a barcode?

If you are in danger, call 911 to receive the most immediate response.

Report Human Trafficking

If you are a victim of human trafficking or have identified someone you think may need help, please contact the National Human Trafficking Resource Center:

Call 888-373-7888
or
Text BEFREE (233733)
or
Chat online with an Advocate
(Available in English and Spanish)
https://humantraffickinghotline.org/chat

This is a national, toll-free hotline, available to answer calls from anywhere in the country, 24-hours a day, 7-days a week, every day of the year. ALL CALLS ARE CONFIDENTIAL.

Please call to:
- Report a tip.
- Connect with anti-trafficking services in your area.
- Request training and technical assistance, general information or specific anti-trafficking resources.

Information obtained from Michigan.gov - Department of Attorney General and HumanTraffickingHotline.org.

About the Author

Pamela Gossiaux is an award-winning journalist, writer and speaker. She has volunteered with many causes for teens over the years and has a passion for human trafficking awareness and prevention. She has a degree in Creative Writing from the University of Michigan, and is the author of the bestselling novel *Mrs. Chartwell and the Cat Burglar*, the *Russo Romantic Mystery Series*, and the chick-lit novel *Good Enough*. Visit her website at PamelaGossiaux.com, follow her on Twitter @ PamelaGossiaux, or sign up for her newsletter.